Too Close To Home

Toni Rocha

Table of Contents

CHAPTER 1

Old Lucy opened her eyes and raised her head as far as the porch timbers would allow. The dawn sky was pale blue and clear, the air chilly despite its being mid-July. Frost glittered on the hoods of cars and tin rooftops of Cooke City, Montana, wedged into a narrow gap of the Beartooth Mountains, a few miles from Yellowstone National Park's eastern gate. As long as it wasn't raining, snowing, sleeting, or hailing, Old Lucy didn't mind.

The big dog pulled herself out from under the porch of the boarded-up wooden building she had slept under that night, shaking off the dirt, cobwebs, and sleepiness. Her breath hung white-vapored in the still air. With a quick stretch and a vigorous shake, she struck out on her morning routine, ambling down a gravel pathway between buildings, heading for the downtown area where she spent her mornings cadging food from restaurants and tourists. In the summer months, Cooke City offered more than enough of both to keep the grizzled old mongrel fed.

Long shadows from the Beartooth Mountains fell across the Hotel 8 parking lot as she trotted through, stopping only once to sniff out the spot where a meandering buffalo had grazed the night before. Old Lucy knew to give the enormous, unpredictable creatures a wide berth, making her smarter than most of the tourists who passed through. She warily crossed the parking lot, keeping a sharp eye out for backing cars and motorcycles.

Old Lucy smelled the aroma of bacon and eggs more strongly as she rounded the corner of the hotel and crossed its drive-through. She stopped for a moment to touch noses with the dog living in the fenced-in area between the hotel and the Bearclaw Bakery. Wagging her tail, she approached two sidewalk tables, one of which was occupied in spite of the morning chill. Just as she arrived, a waitress swung out of the bakery doors, both hands holding plates of steaming breakfast orders.

Old Lucy approached and sat a respectful distance away, her tail smacking the sidewalk.

The waitress noticed her and said, "Hey, old girl! How are you this morning?" before depositing the plates on one of the high tables and disappearing back inside the bakery.

The Bearclaw was a popular breakfast spot for tourists and residents alike, so it was no surprise that, on this frosty morning, the place was hopping. Old Lucy sat by the table and gazed up longingly, a practiced pose that seldom failed to elicit a positive response. And sure enough, the male customer leaned down to toss a hot, fragrant strip of bacon at her feet.

Woofing thanks, she gobbled the bacon and looked up with her dark amber eyes, begging for more. The man laughed, and his companion, a woman, tossed a chunk of freshly baked biscuit slathered with butter to Old Lucy, who caught it deftly and gulped it down.

"Had a lot of practice at that?" the woman said, grinning.

"Oh, she's a regular," the waitress replied as she rushed out of the bakery's front door to refresh the couple's coffee mugs. "Old Lucy has been begging breakfast for as long as I've worked here, and that's going on four years."

The man frowned. "Doesn't she have an owner?"

The waitress paused. "I guess I've never really thought about it. No one has ever said. She's just one of the crazy town characters, goes her own way and doesn't bother anyone."

The woman smiled down at Old Lucy. "She's a sweetie. And it looks as though she's well fed."

The waitress grinned. "That she is. When she's done here, she heads for the Bistro, then the Buns and Beds, and visits a few of the residents. She'll be back around for supper at some of the other restaurants along Main Street later on."

The man frowned. "What kind of dog is she?"

"She looks a bit like my cousin's Australian shepherd," the woman ventured. "But she's huge, way bigger than an average Aussie, and look at those eyes! Gold instead of light blue."

The waitress grinned. "As long as I've been here, the town has speculated on what breeds she is. Some say Australian shepherd, but perhaps with a big dose of wolf."

The man's eyebrows shot up. "Wow, is she safe?"

The waitress looked back over her shoulder as she opened the bakery door. "As long as you don't try to pet her. Old Lucy has very little tolerance for tourists and, especially, kids. It's the fastest way to make her leave, but she's never bitten anyone that I know."

"Well, we must have a photo of Old Lucy to post on Facebook as a memento of our visit," the woman said. "We can boast we had breakfast with a genuine Wild West town character."

The woman snapped a couple of shots and then finished eating. Sensing that the pickings were drying up, Old Lucy drifted off toward the city's center, crossing the street after the Soda Butte Lodge and working her way down the backs of the buildings to the Bistro. The savvy dog didn't like getting close to tourists, so she avoided them by skirting the main street. She sat down on the back porch just outside the door, where a waitress saw her on her way through the side section of the popular restaurant.

"Dog up!" she yelled into the kitchen, where a worker was scraping dishes and loading them into a huge washing machine. The worker grabbed a tin plate piled with scraps and passed it to the waitress. Moments later, the waitress opened the back door with the tin piled with bits of scrambled egg, sausage, and toast scraped from customers' leftovers in front of the old dog.

"There you go, girl," she said as she turned to go back inside.

Old Lucy daintily nibbled at the offering, licking the plate clean. Sighing happily, she ambled further west along the unpaved alley to the western edge of town. One more stop on her list, she knew to cross between buildings, scoot across Main Street, and circle around to the wide back porch of the Sugar Shack, where she was sure to find another pan full of scrapings from customers' plates. The air was heavy with the aroma of the café's signature pastry, yeasty bear claws filled with huckleberry jam instead of apples.

Lucy cleaned the pie plate piled with scraps quickly. Comfortably full, Old Lucy headed for her favorite place in Cooke City, where the only human she had bonded with lived. Set back against the foot of a mountain, a small but charming log cabin with a porch that wrapped around three sides was Old Lucy's habitual next stop. The dog trotted across the lawn, still spotted with frost, and started to climb the steep front steps. Abruptly, she froze, hackles rising, and sniffed the air. Stiff-legged and moving slowly, she continued up the steps and stopped at the top. Lying on the frosted planks was the body of a petite, dark-haired woman. She lay on her right side tilted toward her stomach, her left arm and hand outstretched toward Old Lucy. Behind her feet, the front door hung open.

Old Lucy approached her gingerly, reaching out her snout to touch the woman's hand. It was cold and hard. The iron smell of blood burned Old Lucy's sensitive nose. It splotched the woman's short hair and the back of her plaid flannel shirt. A low growl grew in Old Lucy's throat. She eyed the door. Hesitantly, cautiously on stiff legs, she walked through the door and into the cabin, a place she had never been despite the close bond the woman and dog had forged. Bristling and growling low, the dog padded gingerly through the kitchen, avoiding splatters of blood that trailed from deeper within.

Old Lucy nosed uneasily from kitchen to living room to bedroom, where the scent of the woman who was her friend mingled with that of another. The cabin was cold, and the fireplace and heating system were no match for the bitter, unseasonable mountain air.

Spooked, Old Lucy, slunk back onto the porch and lay beside the woman. She nosed the hand again and leaned closer to lick the woman's cheek. A whine started deep in the old dog's chest and rose, sharp with anguish. Rising to her haunches, she lifted her head to the ice-blue sky as howl after howl of grief burst out and pierced the still air.

Within moments, every dog in Cooke City, Montana, had added its voice to Old Lucy's mournful cry.

CHAPTER 2

"What the hell?"

Lynn Cranston sat up in bed, eyes wide. She glanced at the clock in the dim light. It was barely 7 a.m. She leaned over and shook her husband. "Jake, wake up!"

Jake Cranston raised his head from the pillow and listened. "Sounds like all the hounds of hell have been turned loose," he grumbled.

Lynn pulled back the covers and, wincing at the cold hardwood underfoot, went to the window. She pushed the curtain aside and looked across the yard toward the cabin next door.

"Jake, it's Old Lucy," she murmured.

"What's got her so stirred up?" he muttered.

Lynn peered out of the window and gasped. "Someone is lying on the front porch next door, and the door is open. It looks like Jerianne, and she's not moving. Something's wrong."

Rushing to the closet, Lynn flung open the door and grabbed a robe. She jammed her arms into its sleeves as she shoved her bare feet into slippers and hurried out of the bedroom.

Behind her, Jake was up and dressing. He called out," Lynn, slow down! Be careful!" but she was already running down the stairs from the sleeping loft, through the living room, and into the kitchen. At the back door, her Corgi, Mickie, stood shivering and whining with her nose pressed against the wooden frame.

"Stay!" Lynn commanded, pushing Mickie roughly out of the way. Mickie shot her a reproachful look but backed away and sat.

Unlocking the door, Lynn burst out of the cabin into the icy air and nearly fell as her feet slipped on the frost-covered wooden planks of the wide porch. Grasping the railing and wincing at the wood's cold, clammy feel, she slowed herself down enough to make it safely off the steps before taking off again across the lawn toward the cabin next door.

Old Lucy stopped howling when she saw Lynn coming. Whining with her tail tucked between her legs, she greeted Lynn with an anxious woof, then backed away and sat down by the open door as if she were guarding it. Ignoring the cold flooring, Lynn knelt beside Jerianne and reached out a tentative hand to touch her friend and neighbor. Inches away, she halted the natural motion.

"Don't touch anything," she told herself as she stood up and carefully backed away.

Looking back, she saw Jake coming out of the front door with Mickie on a leash and called out, "Jake, call the sheriff's department."

He yelled back, "What happened?"

Holding back tears, Lynn replied, "It's Jerianne! She's been attacked."

"Do we need an ambulance?" Jake hollered.

Lynn sighed. "No," she answered. "I'm afraid she's dead."

Shaking his head, Jake went back inside and closed the door. Looking across the street and into the town, Lynn could see several residents already headed her way. She walked down the porch steps and stood at the foot, barring the way. When the first ones arrived, she firmly refused to allow them to go any closer.

"There's nothing you can do," she stated. "It's a crime scene, and we're not going to mess it up."

Murmurs greeted her announcement, but no one argued. Even when Edward Sweeny, a retired doctor, joined the growing crowd, he agreed to stand down. Jake eventually joined her, telling everyone that the sheriff's deputies and the Park County coroner were on their way.

"Damn," Dr. Sweeny said. "I can't remember the last time we had a murder in town. And of all people, Jerianne Baker."

Lynn agreed wholeheartedly. Jerianne seemed the least likely person to have made someone so angry that they'd kill her. Barely five-foot tall and slight in build, Jerianne Baker had been Lynn's next-door neighbor for nearly three years. The widowed writer, who supplemented her income by waitressing in Cooke City and nearby Silver Gate, was quiet and reserved, a thoughtful person. Lynn had appreciated Jerianne's wry sense of humor and had read her novels with pleasure.

"What a loss," she mused as she waited with her neighbors for law enforcement.

It took nearly half-an-hour for the nearest Park County sheriff's deputy to arrive. The town folk stood respectful watch until his patrol car pulled into the alley-like street and slowed to a stop without lights or siren. The deputy climbed out of the squad car and, straightening his uniform, loped across the grass to the cabin. Behind Lynn, Old Lucy slowly stood and slunk around the side of the house. Lynn caught the movement out of the corner of one eye but kept her focus on the officer.

"Beartooth Pass was closed last night, still is," he commented, even though everyone in town probably already knew. "We got a ton of snow up there, no traffic coming through from Red Lodge. I had to circle the backroads down from this side of Cody where I was on patrol."

Lynn watched as he carefully climbed the stairs, far enough to see Jerianne's body clearly. Shaking his head, he retreated.

"Best wait until the crime scene guys get here," he said. Pulling a pen and notebook from beneath his jacket, he started asking questions.

"Who found the body?"

Lynn stepped forward. "I did," she responded. "The dog woke us up howling."

The deputy frowned. "And your name is?"

"Lynn Cranston," she answered. "My husband Jake and I were awakened by dogs howling. I saw Jerianne lying on the porch from our bedroom window."

The deputy made a note and asked, "That's the victim's name? Jerianne?"

Jake joined them, saying, "I'm Jake Cranston. Yes, Jerianne Baker. Old Lucy found her and howled. Then every other dog in town howled along with her."

The deputy grunted something close to a laugh. "Never heard that one before."

Jake shook his head. "Never have, either. Don't ever want to again, either."

As the deputy worked his way through the crowd, asking questions, Lynn excused herself and went home. It didn't matter where the investigating officials came from; it would be one-and-a-half to two hours before they could get to Cooke City, depending on road conditions. From Gardiner, they would have to drive through a substantial portion of Yellowstone Park, with narrow roadways blocked by tourists' vehicles slowed or stopped to view wildlife. Even when they arrived, it was unlikely they would share anything they found out anyway. Besides, Lynn realized she was freezing and not adequately dressed for the morning's chill.

In the log A-frame's rustic kitchen, she put on a full pot of strong coffee and pulled eggs, sausage, cheese, and green onions out of the refrigerator. Omelets and toasted English muffins sounded good even though she wasn't certain she could eat them.

With the omelet ingredients prepped for whenever Jake came home, she paced restlessly through the house, distraught. Finally, Lynn filled a mug with coffee and creamer, and carried it into the workshop she and Jake shared, which made up the back half of the large garage attached to their A-frame. Resolutely, Lynn fired up the workroom's Ben Franklyn stove and gathered what she needed to make candles to restock Sweet Stuff, the gift shop she and Jake operated in Cooke City, less than five miles away from Yellowstone's northeast gate.

The couple had left high-pressure professions more than eight years previously and had chosen Cooke City to begin their second careers. Jake was a highly respected craftsman, working in wood and natural elements to create complex pieces that reflected the wilderness and its growing appeal to collectors. Lynn supplemented the shop's Montana-based products with her own brand of candles, candies, and preserves.

Sweet Stuff shared the smaller half of a leased modern pine log cabin building with the Sugar Shack, a breakfast/lunch café, and sold their increasingly popular products online and through mail orders. The shop was scheduled to open at 8 a.m. when their only employee, Ruth Greggory, started work. Monday was normally Lynn's day to go in at 11 a.m. to help handle the noon tourist crowds.

Filling an electric frypan halfway with water, Lynn set the temperature gauge to 180 degrees. She filled a large metal saucepan with pre-chopped wax and set it into the frypan. While the wax melted, she pulled a half-dozen medium-sized glass candle jars from a box and glued pre-made wicks into the base of each one.

When the wax was totally melted, she mixed in oil-based coloring to the perfect shade of reddish-purple and added several drops of huckleberry scent. It took her less than 15 minutes to fill the jars to the brim and trim the wicks. While the candles cooled, Lynn cleaned up her work area. When the candles had cooled enough, she glued on her custom-designed labels and tied a sprig of lavender into a natural-colored raffia bow around the lid of each candle.

Finished with the candle-making project, Lynn carried her mug back into the kitchen, refilled it, and sipped it as she wandered through the house once more, still restless and sad. The busy work had helped, but now time hung heavily in the silent house. She finally walked upstairs to the loft bedroom, where she changed from her robe, pajamas, and slippers into lined corduroy slacks and a long-sleeved sweater, good for a cool weather workday.

For the first time in the seven-plus years they had operated Sweet Stuff, Lynn didn't want to go to work. She dreaded facing the questions and the sympathy. Over and over, her mind returned to the same question: who would want to kill Jerianne?

CHAPTER 3

Cooke City's base population numbered less than 80 year-round residents, but it swelled to hundreds during the summer months as tourists wandered in and out of Yellowstone or drove in over the Beartooth Pass from Red Lodge. And to Lynn, it seemed as if every single one of those residents stopped into Sweet Stuff and the adjoining café, Sugar Shack, that day with something to say or share about Jerianne and the murder investigation.

Across the shop in the Sugar Shack, Lynn heard the murmur from local customers, lower pitched than their usual bantering and laughter. Worse, Ruth's eyes were red-rimmed, and her customary cheerfulness was absent. She greeted Lynn's arrival at 11 a.m. with a flurry of questions that Lynn tried to answer without revealing too much. Ruth kept repeating over and over, "I can't believe this."

Lynn couldn't, either.

When Sugar Shack restaurant owner Connie Russell wandered through the sliding door and into Sweet Stuff after the Sugar Shack had closed at 3 p.m. for the day, her eyes were swollen from crying as well, and her complexion was blotchy.

"I can't believe it. I don't want to believe it. When Jerianne didn't come in for the breakfast shift, I was upset with her. It wasn't like her to miss work," Connie whispered, giving Lynn a hug. "What is this town coming to?"

Lynn replied, "I don't know, Connie. I can't get the horrible sound of Old Lucy's howling and the sight of Jerianne lying there out of my head. And worse, how can I help but believe it was someone who lives in Cooke City who killed her."

Connie frowned. "What makes you so sure of that?" she murmured.

"Think about it," Lynn responded. "The odds of someone who knew her and had a grudge coming into town and spotting her is pretty low. And why would anyone try to break into a house that was obviously occupied? No,   I'm very   much afraid   it's someone we know… and it's making me sick."

Connie turned to Ruth, who said, "I suspect Lynn is right. I mean, it's remotely possible someone came here looking for Jerianne, I suppose. But really, and then how would they have gotten out of town? The pass is closed, and the gate is watched. No, I reluctantly agree with Lynn… it's someone we know."

Her husband Jake came in shortly after 3 p.m. Jake worked on his projects during the morning hours and helped operate Sweet Stuff in the afternoon until closing time at 8 p.m. Lynn welcomed his arrival with a sigh of relief. Ruth finished her work day at 3: 30 p.m.

Unable to take a moment more of the doom and gloom, Lynn left Jake to handle the customers and curiosity seekers. She retreated into the back of the shop, where she began a detailed inventory of the candy stock, making notes on what needed to be replaced. Afterward, she sorted through the day's mail orders and checked the online orders and messages. The back room not only housed stock for sale but also a well-equipped office with a mailing station and Jake's framing table, where he made custom art frames for locals and tourists.

By the end of the afternoon, the stock room had never been so well organized, plus all the mail-in and online orders were packaged and ready to be taken to the post office. Lynn had seldom felt so worn down.

Jake stayed out front, making pot after pot of free coffee and patiently listening while Lynn continued to avoid most questioners. She couldn't bear going over her early morning discovery a single time more. In the infrequent moments when the shop was empty,

Jake rearranged his woodcarvings, handmade picture frames, and pretty much everything else on display in the shop.

"Well, the good news is, we sold a lot today," he commented as they locked up Sweet Stuff at 8 p.m. for the night. "Guilt buying, but hey, who's complaining?"

Lynn gave a weary sigh and leaned against him as they walked home through the deepening twilight. As Jake unlocked their front door, Lynn gazed across the lawns at Jerianne's log cabin, dark and festooned with yellow crime scene tape. No cheery light in the kitchen window, no fragrant woodsmoke from the fireplace chimney. A vagrant thought flitted through Lynn's mind: where was Old Lucy going to go tomorrow morning for her after-breakfast visit? It was no secret that the dog made Jerianne's cabin her last and most beloved stop on her breakfast route. Most days, Old Lucy could be spotted curled up on the front porch or following Jerianne around as she weeded or planted in the yard.

Once inside, Jake filled the teapot with boiling water and set out mugs, cream, and honey. Lynn took two large cranberry orange muffins she had brought from the Sugar Shack out of their box and warmed them in the microwave. She hadn't eaten since they had shared the omelets that morning. Jake gathered everything onto a tray and carried it into the living room. Setting the tray on a small table between two well-padded wooden rockers, he laid a fire in the stone fireplace and lit it. Mickie settled close with her head resting on Lynn's feet.

The familiar, cozy atmosphere contrasted sharply with Lynn's inner turmoil. Over and over, her mind circled back to the moment she saw Jerianne's body on the porch, fully clothed except for shoes. Lynn looked at her feet, shoeless but covered in heavy socks.

"Odd."

Jake looked up from his steaming tea. "What's odd, hun?"

Lynn shook her head. "I keep seeing Jerianne's feet."

"Her feet?" Jake's eyebrows shot up. "Why?"

"She didn't have shoes or socks on. I keep thinking she must have been sitting in front of the fire like we were when someone came to the door," Lynn replied. "And that means it couldn't have been too late because she always works the breakfast shift at Sugar Shack on Mondays, but she was still up."

Jake nodded slowly. "Makes sense."

A long moment passed as the two stared thoughtfully into the flickering fire.

"Jake, did the police say anything was missing from the house?"

"No. And if it had been a robbery, they probably would have said something," he said.

Lynn sighed. "That seems to indicate that it wasn't a stranger."

"How so?"

"Well, a stranger bent on robbery wouldn't have knocked on the door for one thing," Lynn replied. "And for another, Jerianne wouldn't have opened the door to a stranger that late at night."

Jake grunted. "Are you saying you believe it was someone who lives in Cooke City?"

Lynn nodded, adding morosely, "Wouldn't it almost have to be? I mean, what tourist passing through would decide to rob a house and pick Jerianne's? Especially when it must have been obvious that it was occupied and that the person living there was still awake."

Jake thought for a moment, then agreed. "It's equally as unlikely that someone just passing through on vacation would recognize Jerianne and have a grudge against her. The odds would be astronomical."

Jake paused when they heard a knock at the front door. He got up to answer it and returned to the living room, followed closely by a tall, dark-haired man in a suit and tie.

"Good evening, Mrs. Cranston," he said. "I'm Jeffrey Palmer, an investigative detective with the sheriff's office. I was wondering if you would help us out with something."

Lynn set her tea mug down and rose from the chair. "Certainly," she said.

"Were you ever inside Ms. Baker's home?"

"Yes, I was, many times," Lynn confirmed.

"Would you be willing to walk through the victim's home and see if anything is missing?" he asked.

"Of course. Let me put my shoes and jacket on, and I'll go over there with you right now," Lynn said.

As she went to get ready, Jake turned to the detective. "How is the investigation going?"

"Slow," the obviously weary officer replied. "We know no one came into Cooke City or left it over Beartooth Pass during the night because it was closed. And we're fairly sure only a few cars came into Cooke City from Yellowstone. We are checking with the gate to learn how many cars left early this morning and went into the park. They should have a fairly comprehensive list, hopefully a short one."

Lynn rejoined them, and they walked across the lawn together. Lynn hesitated, but only for a moment, before climbing the steep steps to the front door of Jerianne's cabin. Inside, it was noticeably cool. Lynn felt the chill settle into her and shivered.

"Just look around, but don't touch anything," Palmer said. "We have fingerprinted and swept the place for evidence, but it's still a protected crime scene."

Redundant, Lynn thought because she had no intention of touching a single thing in the cabin. Silently and slowly, Lynn walked through the open layout, including the kitchen, dining area, and living room that made up the front of the cabin, carefully avoiding the dark blood spatters. Down a short hall, she looked into the bedroom and bath but did not enter either room.

All around her were memories of her friend: Jerianne's simple, uncluttered style, homey touches like the quilts and afghans she loved, and Native American pottery in soft pastels that complimented the warm, grainy woods of the floors and walls.

"I seldom was in those rooms," she explained as she returned to the main living area. Lynn stood in the center of the dining space and focused all her attention as she turned in a full circle. Jerianne's pared-down décor made it easy to see what was missing.

"I don't see Jerianne's laptop, nor do I see her cell phone."

Palmer frowned. "Cell phone? They don't work well here, do they?"

"Not always, but Jerianne had one for when she traveled while working on a novel or writing assignment. She did research and wrote on her laptop."

Palmer made notes as Lynn continued.

"The Wi-Fi here is spotty. It's constantly cutting out, sometimes working one minute and not the next," Lynn explained. "Jerianne jokingly complained about that a lot because it made things difficult when she couldn't get a manuscript or article sent to an editor by the deadline. She'd get so frustrated."

Tears began to run down Lynn's face, and Jake, who was standing outside at the foot of the porch steps, called up, "Lynn, why don't we go back home now."

Palmer nodded. "Nothing else?"

"No."

Palmer walked with them to their front door, then thanked Lynn and said goodnight. As the unmarked cruiser slowly moved off down the narrow unpaved street, Lynn gratefully went back into her warm, softly lit home.

"That pretty much confirms what I believe," she said softly.

"That it was someone who lives here?"

"Yes."

Jake shook his head sadly. "I believe it, but I really hate to believe it."

Lynn sighed deeply. "And you know what's worse? We came here partially to get away from this sort of big city violence. I have been so happy here, so comfortable. We've made good friends here. And now? Believing someone we know, someone we've accepted as a neighbor and friend, might have killed one of us? Eight years, and it feels as if we are right back where we started."

CHAPTER 4

The next morning, Lynn glanced out the kitchen window and was saddened to see Old Lucy lying on Jerianne's porch. A wave of sorrow swept through her again for the loss of a good friend. She opened the refrigerator and took out shredded cheese and some cooked chicken she had minced for sandwiches, along with an egg that she scrambled in a small bowl. Pouring all of the food into a frying pan, she cooked it and let it cool briefly while she put on her jacket and changed slippers for shoes.

"I'm going over to Jerianne's," she called out to Jake as she unlocked the living room door.

He came to the doorway that led to the workshop area. "And why are you doing that?"

"Old Lucy is there," she replied. "I'm taking her some breakfast."

Jake nodded absently. He was deeply involved in a new project incorporating an impressive pair of elk horns a friend had brought in from a pack trip into the Beartooth Mountains earlier in the week.

Lynn crossed the yards and called out to Old Lucy, who just wagged her tail but remained on the porch, watching her warily. Lynn sighed.

Carefully, minding where she stepped, she approached and pushed the paper plate with the food on it through the bars of the porch and close to the old dog. Old Lucy sniffed at the food and then daintily picked at it. Lynn returned home and prepared for another day at Sweet Stuff.

Opening the kitchen door with an armload of the newly made candles scented with huckleberry from the morning before, she nearly tripped over Old Lucy. The dog leaped up and out of the way.

"Goodness! You scared me," Lynn gently scolded the dog.

Old Lucy wagged her tail and seemed to grin up at her. Lynn grinned back. She loaded a small, two-wheeled pull cart with the candles and started down the steps with Old Lucy following closely behind. Together, they walked the few blocks to Sweet Stuff, greeting a few early morning resident walkers and tourists already out on Cooke City's main street. The day was warming quickly, and sunlight glittered off the mountaintops.

At the shop, Lynn parked the cart beside a bench and unlocked the door. It was Ruth's day off, so she would be working alone until Jake came in at 3 p.m. As she went inside, she saw Old Lucy settle down on the boardwalk on the other side of the door from the customer bench in a patch of sunlight.

"Hmmm," Lynn thought as she began to re-align several sizes of glass jar candles on the display shelves to make room for the new ones. "Apparently, I've been adopted."

It felt good to think she could do something positive about a bad situation. Lynn smiled as she rearranged the candles to accommodate the new batch, dusting the shelves as she worked. Finished with that project, she was carrying the empty boxes back into the storage area when the sleigh bells over the shop door jingled. Looking back over her shoulder, she saw Winnie Fredericks coming inside.

"I'll be with you in a minute, Winnie," Lynn called out.

"No problem," Winnie replied. "Warmer today."

"Yes, it is," Lynn agreed as she came back into the shop area. "I just brought in some new candles you might like."

Winnie smiled, and her eyes lit up. "You know me well," she said. "Oh, huckleberry… nice. I love the scent of them when I can get enough to make jam. Not very many get this far from the western part of the state."

Picking up one of the medium candle jars, she carried it to the checkout station and pulled out her wallet. "You know," she murmured as she counted out enough bills to pay, "there's talk Jerianne Baker did a lot of research on folks living here in the Cooke City area."

Lynn blinked. "What do you mean?"

"Well, some are speculating that she was digging into a few folks who perhaps didn't want their past dug up. They're speculating that she was writing a new novel and that somehow, they were going to be part of the plot."

Lynn shook her head. "Somehow, I can't imagine Jerianne doing that."

"Me, either, but you know how people talk," Winnie replied. "Even if it weren't true, and I doubt it was, that could be a powerful motive."

"Really?"

Winnie settled the candle in one of Sweet Stuff's distinctive rose-colored bags. "Yep, I mean, why would folks choose to move way out here? No cell phone service, practically no Internet, no close police presence, and we all tend to mind our own business. Perfect place to get away from it all, if you have reason to get away from anything at all."

Winnie pointedly looked across the shop into the Sugar Shack. Lynn's left eyebrow rose. Winnie saw it.

"Maybe not that last one so much, but we do tend to talk more about what happens here, not go rooting around into what happened before a person moved here," Winnie added.

Lynn allowed that this was so. And if Jerianne had been researching someone in town, it would explain why her laptop and cell phone had disappeared, most likely never to be found again.

After all, with thousands of square miles of mountain wilderness surrounding Cooke City, plus all the potential dumping places in Yellowstone's nearly inaccessible areas, a laptop and phone would be easy enough to permanently lose. On the other hand, Lynn wondered if maybe it was something that had happened in Cooke City, and Jerianne had found out about it. This notion tallied with her growing belief that it was someone who had lived in town for a while.

"And where's that handsome husband of yours this morning," Winnie commented, interrupting her thoughts.

"He's working on a new piece. Jeff Broghan brought him some elk horn from his last pack trip," Lynn replied distractedly.

"I'll look forward to seeing that, even if I can't afford to buy one of his works," Winnie said. "I consider Sweet Stuff to be as much a western-themed museum as a retail shop."

Lynn was used to hearing this about Jake's art. Few realized how much he poured into each piece, the long hours of carving, sanding, hand-rubbing, and the painstakingly slow process of layering paint and stain so it enhanced the fine wood grain instead of masking it. The entire back wall of Sweet Stuff's shop area held Jake's frameable and hangable art, with shelves and stands of his sculptures interspersed beneath.

"Oh, and I see Old Lucy has switched allegiance," Winnie continued. "Are you going to lay claim to her? I heard the sheriff's patrol was fixing to round her up since no one has stepped up to own her."

The thought of the old dog, a long-standing resident of the town whom everyone treated as a friend, being impounded shook her.

"I'm talking to Jake about adopting her," Lynn said, thinking, well, it was true; she would be as soon as he came in. On his next trip to Cody for supplies, Jake could easily pick up a collar and some doggie dishes.

"Good to hear. Wonder what Mickie will think of that?" Winnie nodded. Lynn grinned. "I suspect she'll fall back on her usual judgmental attitude. Have a good day."

"You, too," Winnie called back as she left the shop.

Lynn went back into the storage area and rummaged around, looking for something to use as a water dish for Old Lucy. She found a battered enamel bowl and filled it from the sink in the store's bathroom. Outside, Old Lucy gratefully lapped at the cold water. The day was definitely warming up. Up Main Street, Lynn could see a solid line of parked cars and tourists wandering back and forth across it, from shops to restaurants. The rest of the day went by quickly and profitably.

Old Lucy stayed by the store's door pretty much all day long. When the long shadows of twilight began to fall from the mountains, she leisurely strolled across the highway and began her routine of cadging dinner. Dozens of diners filled the outdoor tables at the Bistro and the Bearclaw Café. Lynn was pretty sure Old Lucy wouldn't go hungry that night, at least, and wasn't sure she would come back to the cabin later. When she locked up for the night, Old Lucy was nowhere in sight.

Jake hadn't come for the afternoon shift; Lynn was used to his habit of getting so deeply involved in a project that he forgot the time. Lynn hiked back up the slope toward home alone and was disconcerted to see the sheriff's squad car parked in front. Sure enough, Detective Palmer was sitting on the front porch chatting with Jake. Mickie was curled up next to Jake's rocker.

"Good evening, Mrs. Cranston," he greeted her. "Your husband and I were just talking about the dog."

Lynn glanced pointedly at Jake and said, "We have been thinking we would officially adopt her."

Both of Jake's eyebrows flew up. Lynn ignored it.

"Really?" Palmer responded.

"Really?" Jake echoed, a bemused look on his face.

"Old Lucy usually spent most of the day on Jerianne's front porch and we all pretty much considered her to be Jerianne's dog," Lynn continued determinedly. "Truth is, no one knows who Old Lucy's owner is, or was for that matter. But now, in light of what's happened…" Lynn's voice trailed off.

"I guess that settles it. I am willing to report that you own Old Lucy, but I expect you to get her licensed, collared, and given updated rabies shots pronto," he said sternly. A small smile twitching at the corner of his mouth belied his gruffness.

"I'm curious," he continued. "Heard anything around town?"

Lynn blinked back, surprise. "Yes, as a matter of fact. One of my customers said there's speculation that Jerianne was researching people in town and learned a few things that someone might not want to be made public."

"You wouldn't want to tell me who?"

Lynn shook her head. "It would be idle gossip or speculation," she said. "Besides, the person didn't name names."

Palmer grunted. "That would explain the missing computer and phone. It would be easy to do a search to see what she had been hunting. At least it would explain the speculation, but we held that information back. You didn't say anything about it, did you?

Lynn shook her head vehemently. "No, I did not."

Palmer was silent for a moment. "Interesting," he finally muttered. "Either someone is really good at guessing, or that notion was started by someone who knows something and has gone fishing."

Lynn shivered. Before she could respond, Old Lucy drifted out of the evening shadows, padded up the porch steps, and, with a satisfied sigh, plunked down at Lynn's feet. Jake sighed. Mickie raised her head, startled, and gave the old dog one of her finest judgmental glares. Lynn tried to hide a grin and failed utterly.

Palmer didn't even try. He said his goodbyes with a wide smile. Jake and Lynn went inside, Lynn holding the door and calling Old Lucy inside with them. After a slight hesitation, the dog obeyed. Once the door was closed and locked, she curled up on the rug in front of it and laid her head on her paws with a contented sigh. Mickie studied Old Lucy with a puzzled tilt of her head. Then she laid down on the hardwood floor a few feet away, her back to the intruder.

"I can't bear to think of her in the dog pound," Lynn said before Jake had a chance to protest.

"Did you think about how we were going to convince her to get vaccinated?" Jake muttered. "I'm not even going to think about loading her in the SUV. We'll have to call the vet in from Red Lodge."

Lynn sighed. "I know it will be expensive, but…"

"I know. And all things considered, it might not be a bad idea to have her here," Jake returned. "We apparently have a killer in Cooke City."

CHAPTER 5

Days passed and talk died down some. By Friday, the police presence had abated and a bit of the tension eased. However, Lynn felt the change in the city's atmosphere, as did everyone else, an undercurrent of unease that hadn't been there before. People looked at each other differently, not quite as open nor as trusting with those hadn't they come to know well.

Sad, Lynn thought as she restocked Sweet Stuff's candy shelves with her rum fudge truffles, a specialty candy she made and sold successfully both in the shop and online.

The door chimes brought Lynn from the back room with an armload of bagged, huckleberry-flavored saltwater taffy she had purchased in bulk from a popular candy store in Phillipsburg, in the western part of Montana. Just inside the door, Winnie was peering out and down at Old Lucy, who one again had taken up residence by the shop door. Lynn had let the old dog out of the cabin early that morning and smiled to see her trot off on her regular breakfast run.

"Seems like you really have been adopted. I see she has a new collar," Winnie said with a wide grin.

"Yes, we have," Lynn smiled back. "But she still made her rounds this morning. One thing, we won't have to feed her much."

Winnie laughed. "That's for sure. She's getting so much sympathy you may need to put her on a diet."

Lynn lined her signature pink and white candy bags up neatly in a display bin. "What can I do for you this morning?"

Winnie didn't hesitate. "Seems like the cops aren't doing much about Jerianne's murder," she stated. "Haven't seen that Palmer fellow around for a couple of days."

Lynn shook her head. "What have you heard?"

"Talk. Are they checking who went in and out of the park the night Jerianne died?" Winnie replied. "I haven't heard anything about results, of course. Those guys keep things pretty close to their vests. Even so, it's possible for someone to get through unseen, I suppose, even hike through."

"Hmmmm," Lynn leaned on the counter and gazed out the window. "Cold as it was, with the pass closed, there couldn't have been much traffic," she murmured. "Folks would have been afraid of the road conditions. I wouldn't want to be driving some of the park's roads in iffy weather."

From the far end of the shop, where she was dusting shelves, Ruth added her two cents worth.

"I don't like driving them in any weather," she called out. "And that goes for a lot of other roads around here."

Everyone in town knew Yellowstone Park's roadways… narrow, some less than 16 feet across for both lanes, with little or no shoulder room. Many of the roads didn't have railings, either, and the drops were enough to scare drivers on a good day. Traffic jams were frequent. Tourists stopped in the middle of the road to gawk at wildlife, everything from buffalo to elk to bear or moose, who were just as often also on the road.

"Me, either. And if it had been someone in town, they would be conspicuous by their absence," Lynn commented. "Anyone we know missing?"

Winnie frowned and shook her head, "No one, I noticed. All the usual suspects are still here."

Lynn burst out laughing. "Oh, Winnie, listen to us," she giggled. "We sound like a couple of snoopy old women in one of those smarmy Agatha Christy books like Miss Marple."

Winnie snorted. "Actually, that's not a bad idea."

Startled, Lynn stared at her. "What do you mean?"

"Well," Winnie drawled. "We could launch our own investigation. I mean, we know the town as well or better than anyone from the outside, including our local law enforcement."

Lynn nearly groaned out loud. "Winnie, that's not a good idea. I mean, we're looking at someone who killed Jerianne, possibly to keep her from exposing him or her. Just think what might happen if this person learned we were snooping around."

Winnie sighed. "I knew you'd say that. But Lynn, I hate what this has done to the town. People look over their shoulders and wonder who they know who could or would do such a terrible thing. It could be a neighbor, a customer, someone you see every morning sipping coffee at the Soda Butte Lodge, eating dinner at the Bistro, anyone."

Secretly, Lynn agreed but didn't want to encourage Winnie. Someone who felt it expedient to kill once would not likely hesitate to do it again if he or she felt threatened.

"Winnie, promise you won't do anything stupid," Lynn urged her friend.

Winnie hedged. "Well, okay… maybe," she finally said.

As she watched as Winnie crossed the Sweet Stuff shop and went through the double sliding doors into the Sugar Shack where she bellied up to the coffee bar, ordered one of the café's famous huckleberry bearclaws, and began an animated conversation with the café owner, Connie. Lynn felt unsettled. Winnie was headstrong and opinionated, a combination that could lead to trouble.

At home that night, Lynn and Jake fried fresh trout with fried potatoes and onions. Old Lucy snoozed on the rug in front of the door. Mickie edged closer to Old Lucy and curled up on the kitchen floor nearby. Inevitably, the conversation focused on Winnie and her determination to investigate.

"Not a good idea," was Jake's immediate reaction. "And I hope you didn't encourage her. Whoever did this to Jerianne is dangerous."

Lynn nodded. "I did. But you know Winnie."

"Yeah, I do," Jake replied grimly. "I'm afraid for her."

"Me, too." Lynn paused to rinse the dishes and empty the dishpan. "I have a bad feeling about all this."

"What do you mean?"

Lynn sighed. "Just… as if this is the beginning of something even more tragic. Hope I'm wrong."

"Me, too," agreed Jake.

CHAPTER 6

Lynn looked up from arranging a new shipment of western wildlife souvenirs as two familiar Cooke City residents came into Sweet Stuff. Helen Gable and Judith Wilson were sisters who spent most of their daytime hours together while their respective husbands worked. They strolled through several aisles, browsing and chatting. From her place near the back of the shop, she could hear them murmuring softly but couldn't quite catch their words. It wasn't until they came to the counter to pay for their purchases that she got an earful.

"Lynn, did you hear? Winnie Fredricks has disappeared," Helen announced.

Lynn turned from the cash register with a jerk. "What do you mean, disappeared?"

"Well," Judith added, "no one has seen her since yesterday afternoon. Her neighbor, Julie Harper, said she knocked on Winnie's door this morning because she could hear Winnie's cat yowling inside."

Lynn frowned. "Did Julie call the sheriff's department to do a welfare check?"

Both women shook their heads. "I don't think so," Judith ventured as she put several items down on the checkout counter.

Neither of the women said more about Winnie's odd absence as they paid for their purchases and left. Lynn watched them go, and a deep uneasiness overtook her. Jake was in the stock room, unpacking more wildlife items. Lynn poked her head into the stock area and told him what she had just heard.

"I'm going over to Winnie's to take a look," she said.

Jake stood up and dusted off his hands. "I'm coming with you. No argument."

Lynn smiled. "I was actually hoping you'd say that."

It was after 3 p.m., and Ruth had gone home for the day. They locked up Sweet Stuff, hung a back-soon sign on the door, and walked the few blocks to Winnie's home. As they neared the front door, both could clearly hear a cat meowing loudly. Then, they could see a little Siamese pawing at the front door window.

"Not a good sign," Jake muttered.

He checked the front door and found it securely locked. Together, they walked around to the back porch and tested that door. It too was locked.

"What do we do now?" Lynn asked.

Jake hesitated, then decided, "We go back to the shop and call Palmer," he stated. "And we wait there until he or someone from the sheriff's department can come to investigate."

As they turned to go, Julie came out on her porch and called out to them, obviously agitated.

"I haven't seen Winnie since yesterday late afternoon when she left in her car," she told them. "That's so unusual, and she dotes on that cat. I can't imagine her leaving without making some kind of arrangement for Miss Elsie. Winnie has had that cat for 17 years."

Julie offered to let Jake use her landline. Lynn made casual conversation with her, keeping one ear cocked to hear what Jake was saying on the phone. She was relieved when it became evident that he was talking to Detective Palmer and not someone who might not be familiar with the case.

"Palmer is on his way," Jake said as he hung up. "I told him Winnie was nosing around, and he's concerned, too. He said normally they'd send a deputy for a welfare check, but in this case, he's worried."

Lynn nodded. "Should we stay?"

"I'll stay," Jake answered. "Why don't you go back and open up again? There's no reason for both of us to be here when he arrives."

Reluctantly, Lynn agreed and left. Walking back to the shop in a daze, she nearly tripped over Old Lucy, who had risen from her now-familiar place next to the door.

"Oooh, Lucy!" Lynn exclaimed, reaching down to pat the dog's warm head gently. Lucy's tail wagged tentatively. "It's okay, girl."

The next two hours passed slowly as Lynn alternated between waiting on customers and restlessly rearranging shelves. With a sigh of relief mingled with anxiety, she welcomed the sight of Jake coming down the sidewalk. He came in with a slight shake of his head and waited until Lynn finished with a customer before answering her unspoken questions.

"So, what did Palmer find?"

Jake replied, "Nothing. The house looked as if Winnie had just stepped out for a bit. Nothing was disturbed, and her purse was gone, but everything else was pretty much exactly as the neighbor said; it was the last time she dropped by."

Lynn frowned. "So, how long has it been since the neighbor saw her?"

"Yesterday, she thinks," Jake replied. "The mail from yesterday is still in the box, so it seems like that's a good guess. But Winnie's car is gone, so wherever she went, it wasn't in town."

Jake and Lynn both gazed off into space for a long moment.

"Do you suppose she drove over to Silver Gate?" Lynn finally murmured.

"Why would she do that?"

"Because Jerianne waitressed in one of the restaurants there," Lynn said. "She could have decided to snoop around over there."

"You've got a point," Jake responded, reaching for the landline phone.

While Jake called Det. Palmer suggested he look for Winnie's car in Silver Gate; Lynn watched as another customer, a tall, lanky man she had seen around town for a few summers, entered the shop. Cooke City attracted a small but dedicated number of summer residents who spent the warm months in rentals. This summer-timer had ginger hair generously sprinkled with gray, distant green-gray eyes and an off-putting demeanor.

Lynn wasn't entirely positive, but she thought the man's name was Jeremy Walsh. Moments later, another summer-timer, a slim, dark-haired fellow with a perpetual smile, joined the first customer. Chad… something, Lynn thought to herself. Together, they wandered through Sweet Stuff, finally coming to the checkout counter with one of Lynn's new huckleberry container candles and a box of truffles.

"Beautiful store you have here," Chad commented as Lynn tried to recall if they had ever been in Sweet Stuff before. "You don't find huckleberries nearby, do you?"

"No, they grow farther west of here as a rule, but you can find some in the park," Lynn replied, packaging up their purchases.

"I hear the bears love them," the man continued.

"Yes, they do," Lynn agreed. "If you come across a road blocked with traffic in the park, there is a good chance it's a stand of huckleberry bushes with a bear inside."

Chad laughed while his taller companion glanced at him with what looked to Lynn like an irritated frown and took out his wallet.

As Jeremy counted out the money, he casually stated, "Lots of excitement around town today."

Lynn blinked at the sudden change in subject. There was something about Jeremy that was off-putting, Lynn thought as she put the money in the till and closed it. He had a stillness about him that felt as if something was coiled up deep inside, ready to strike.

"In what way?" Jake queried, coming into the shop from the back room.

"Well, they're all talking about an older woman's disappearance," Chad replied. "I guess she was a long-time resident. Sad, but as wild as the countryside is around here, I suppose that can happen occasionally."

This time, Jeremy turned and glared at his companion.

"Really, Chad," he murmured in a deep, cultured voice.

Chad glanced at him with a quirky smile. "Guess it's time for lunch," he continued. "Nice to shop with you."

Without further comment, the two turned and left the shop. Jake stared after them with an odd expression.

"What?"

"I don't like what I just heard," he mused.

"And what was that?" Lynn asked.

"That man referred to Winnie in the past tense. He said 'was' when there's no reason to suspect that anything bad has happened to her or that she's no longer with us," Jake answered.

"True," Lynn said thoughtfully. "All though it could have been a slip of the tongue."

Jake shrugged. "I suppose it could have."

More than an hour had passed since Jake had called Palmer and waited for him to arrive. That time passed in restless activity aimed at keeping Lynn's and Jake's minds off what might have happened to Winnie. At this rate, Sweet Stuff will be the best shape it's ever been, Lynn mused. When the Sweet Stuff's door opened, and both looked up from their cleaning and restocking efforts, they were relieved to see Palmer stride inside. His face was grim.

"We found Mrs. Fredrick's car in Silver Gate exactly where you suggested," he announced without preamble. "It implies that someone may have taken her somewhere."

Lynn sighed. "That can't be good."

Palmer agreed. "No, it can't, especially with Yellowstone Gate so close by. We're checking the park gate to see if she was seen going in with anyone. But with literally thousands of square miles of mountains and forests, I'm hoping she's somewhere we can find her."

Outside of Cooke City and Silver Gate, the entryway to the eastern border of Yellowstone National Park, the population was sparse and scattered. Inside Yellowstone, away from the busy tourist areas and limited paved roadways, a vast region to the southeast lay unreachable by vehicle. Trailheads marked hiking trails that meandered away from pull-off parking lots and deep into the trackless wilderness, populated with wild animals and little else. Finding a person there, dead or alive, seemed a near impossibility without some kind of clue as to where he or she might be. A person who had a rudimentary knowledge of the area would have little trouble finding places to stash unwanted things such as laptops, cell phones, and bodies.

Lynn's eyes filled with tears. "Oh, god, why didn't you listen to me?" she whispered. Looking up, she saw a quizzical expression on Palmer's face. "I told her not to snoop around, that it would be dangerous because one person is already dead. I'm afraid she didn't take it seriously."

Jake put his arm around Lynn's shoulders and gave her a brief squeeze.

"I'm afraid you're right," he said.

CHAPTER 7

Winnie Fredricks slowly opened her eyes. A stab of bright light sent a bolt of sharp pain through her head. She moaned, closed her eyes, and laid still until the pain subsided. She could feel the heat on her face. Sun or something else, she wondered vaguely.

Carefully lifting her right arm, she shielded her face with her hand and tried opening her eyes again, blinking rapidly. This time, the pain was a bit milder. Winnie tried turning her head and found she could without causing more discomfort. She was lying on her back on dirt, a lumpy, rutted area dotted with rocks and scrubby grass. Beyond, she could see boulders rising into the sun. She closed her eyes and took stock.

Okay, I'm outdoors in the sun, she told herself. I don't hear people or much of anything, for that matter. I must be out of town, maybe at a campsite or in a parking area. It's warm, so it must be around midday.

Taking a deep breath, Winnie eased onto her left side and studied the area. More rocks and brush, not much sign of human occupation; a few old tire tracks, maybe. Steeling herself for more pain, Winnie slowly pushed into an upright position. A wave of dizziness caused her to close her eyes for a long minute, but she remained upright, held up by a shaky left arm.

"I need something to help me stand," she said out loud.

Turning her head carefully, she spotted the rotted-out stump of a small tree that just might be tall enough, but it was several yards away. Taking another deep breath, Winnie carefully maneuvered herself onto her hands and knees. It took time and effort, leaving Winnie frozen in position until she felt strong enough to move. Then she began a lurching crawl toward the tree stump. After what felt like ages, her knees and unprotected hands stinging from hot sand and sharp stones, she reached the tree and, hand over hand, slowly and painfully pulled herself upright. Her efforts resulted in another dizzy spell. Winnie closed her eyes and held on tightly until that passed.

"Okay, now what? I'm up, but I'm afraid to try to walk without some sort of support," she muttered.

Winnie began searching the immediate area for something she could use to help her balance. Not far away lay a sturdy-looking branch. But how to reach it without falling? After what seemed like an eternity, Winnie decided it would be best to crawl over to the stick and drag it back to the tree. It wasn't that far, and getting down on all fours again was easier than she had expected it to be.

Stick in hand, she crawled back to the tree and pulled herself up. Several minutes passed while Winnie rested and her breathing slowed, Then, with the aid of the stick cane, she took a few tentative steps and stopped to more thoroughly evaluate her surroundings. As she turned toward the pile of jumbled boulders, a sound caught her attention. Winnie started to grin.

"I know that sound," she whispered. "Water."

Suddenly aware of her dry mouth and itchy eyes, Winnie stumbled toward the welcome sound of a tiny stream of snow runoff that meandered between the boulders and filled a small pool within a narrow cleft between the rocks. It wasn't easy, but Winnie used the stick and tall rocks to ease her way through to the pool, where she once again dropped to her hands and knees. She scooped up the brackish water and drank.

"Not too much at a time," she cautioned herself.

But there was no limit to the cool water she splashed on her face, rinsing off her eyes and then pouring it all over her head. Winnie gently poured water down the back of her head, the source of continued pain. She winced when she touched it, sucking in her breath in a sharp hiss.

"Not good," she murmured.

Feeling stronger, Winnie found a relatively comfortable spot to sit where she could easily reach the water and took stock.

"The good news is… I know exactly where I am," she said wryly. "The bad news is… I know exactly where I am."

The person who had assaulted and abducted Winnie must not have known that when she was married to her late husband, David, they had spent almost every weekend hiking, camping, and fishing. Winnie was familiar with a great deal more of the region surrounding Cooke City than the average resident. Thus, the attacker had made a mistake… dumping her in a place she knew well: an off-the-grid campsite high on one of the mountains overlooking the city with a breath-taking view of the magnificent scenery. It was reached by a dirt track that no one would reasonably call a road: a one-lane, two-rut road up the mountain. Someone had known it was there, someone who obviously lived in Cooke City or nearby. Did he… or was it she?... dump her there to die?

"If this person killed Jerianne, why didn't they just kill me, too?" Winnie wondered. "Why me? Did I find out something they didn't want anyone to know?"

And why couldn't she remember anything clearly, Winnie silently added. She remembered driving over to the gateway and then parking her car outside the supper club where Jerianne had worked. But she couldn't remember anything after that.

"It will come back to me. It has to come back," Winnie told herself.

But for now, Winnie knew she had a major challenge ahead. It was at least 12 miles from the old campsite to the main highway east of Cooke City. The odds of anyone driving up there any time soon were poor to none. That meant Winnie had a long, brutal hike ahead of her. She shaded her eyes and gazed up at the sky. The sun's position seems to indicate it was early afternoon.

Winnie took another half-hour to repeatedly drink her fill, knowing there was no way she could take water with her. Feeling stronger and more stable, she leaned on her stick cane and walked to the head of the rutted road.

"Well, there's one thing in my favor," she muttered. "It's all downhill from here."

CHAPTER 8

Lynn sat on the wide back porch in the bright sunlight that streamed between two of the town's surrounding mountains, her feet propped on another chair. With a warm hand on her shoulder, she looked up to see Jake standing over her with a fresh cup of coffee. She smiled her thanks, then continued to gaze in the general direction of Jerianne's cabin.

"What?"

Lynn sighed. "It's been almost two days and no sign of Winnie," she murmured. "I can't … won't believe she is gone."

Jake grunted softly. "I can't and won't believe it, either. This seems so surreal. We have lived here peacefully for years, and now everything feels strange."

Lynn hesitated for a moment and then ventured, "And there's something else that's bothering me."

"What's that, hon?" Jake replied.

"Remember the other day when those two men came into the store? I don't recall them shopping with us before," Lynn said. "And more, they appear to have joined the regulars in the Sugar Shack pretty much daily, but I don't believe they did before Jerianne…"

Jake nodded, mostly to himself because Lynn was still gazing off into near space. "I'm not usually there while the Sugar Shack is open, so I don't know for sure, but if they changed their habits now, I would be a bit suspicious, too. Are one or both of them keeping an ear out for information, I wonder?"

Lynn nodded in return. "That's what I was thinking. And I believe we're missing something here."

Jake agreed. "Right, like a possible connection between one or both of the men and Jerianne. Have you heard anything like that?"

Once again, Lynn was silent for a moment. "No, but remember, Jerianne worked in more than one restaurant. Maybe it's connected to that fancy supper club in Silver Gate. She worked there nights several times a week, including the night she was killed."

Jake added, "Yes, and that's where Winnie's car was found."

Lynn twisted in her chair to look at Jake. "So, what can we do without endangering ourselves to check it out."

Jake opened his mouth to refuse but then paused. "I suppose we could go out to dinner tonight. Just a couple of Cooke City old-timers trying out a new place to eat out."

Lynn smiled. "That would work, and there's two of us so it's not likely someone would try anything, right?"

"They had better not," Jake growled.

Lynn managed a weak smile.

Old Lucy drifted out of the shadows and up onto the porch. She drank from the metal bowl set beside the doorway and settled with a sigh onto the planks near Lynn's feet. Mickie, who had been snoozing under the nearby table, raised her head and assessed the situation.

"What do you think? Are they becoming friends and family, or is Mickie trying to decide if there's a threat?" Jake wondered.

Lynn grinned. "Well, I don't see any raised hackles, snarky looks… well, maybe Mickie… or hear any growling, so I think for now it's a standoff. Do you suppose Lucy's hungry?"

Jake snorted a sharp laugh. "Not likely. The weather's perfect, and the pickings are ripe. But you could try."

Lynn got up and went into the cabin, returning with some scraps of fried trout from last night's supper. She set them down next to Old Lucy, who sniffed at them appreciatively and then nibbled daintily. Mickie gazed at the other dog but didn't appear to be overly concerned. The Corgie didn't even bother to get up and check the scraps out. Probably a good thing, Lynn thought.

After they locked up the Sweet Shop up at 8 p.m. that evening, Lynn and Jake drove over to Silver Gate and parked in the crowded lot that served the Timberline Inn, an upscale pseudo western supper club housed in an equally fantastical building of dark timber, rough natural stone, and huge plate glass windows that glowed with golden light. It loomed over the landscape, enormous and enormously popular with tourists, Lynn knew from gossip heard around the Sweet Shop and Sugar Shack.

Inside, a hostess led them to a window overlooking a broad lawn bordered by dark evergreens and lit here and there with ground lights. The tables were covered in crisp white linen and set with sparkling silver and glass. Candles gleamed at every table. One side of the open format was designed for dining, while the other side, almost half the area raised by two steps to a different level, held a huge, rugged wooden bar and dozens of counter-level tables filled with customers. The square table was set in one corner of the wall, which allowed them to sit next to each other. At the same time, both faced the vast dining room.

"Humph," Jake murmured after they place their drink order.

"What?"

"Hail, hail, the gang's all here," he replied cryptically.

Casually, Lynn turned her head to see what Jake was seeing from his angle.

"All the usual suspects," she whispered, and Jake snorted.

At one end of the busy bar, at tables pulled together, they could see Jeremy and his friend Chad, plus several regular customers from the Sugar Shack. Turning back to Jake, she abruptly stopped and stared at someone seated alone several feet down the bar from the noisy group and shielded by bar customers.

"Jake, look about seven stools to the left of where Jeremy's group is sitting. Isn't that Ruth?"

Jake gazed over at the bar and nodded. "You mean behind that woman in the blue dress? How odd, Ruth sitting there alone like that, not part of the favored few, apparently."

Lynn frowned. "What do you mean?"

"Group dynamics," Jake replied. "Jeremy is the obvious center around which the rest are gathered. It's as if he were holding court."

Lynn shook her head. "Don't you mean Chad, the chatty one?"

Jake snorted. "No, not the delicious Chad," he replied, sarcasm dripping in his tone. At Lynn's incredulous look, he continued, "I got the look the other day."

Lynn sighed. Jake was handsome, and she was used to women being attracted to him. Somehow, she hadn't noticed the same attraction emanating from men. Before she could respond, the waiter returned to take their dinner orders. The menu was fashionably simple, only a dozen choices but they reflected the best of the west, Lynn decided. The prices did, too.

Jake ordered a cowboy steak, huge by any standards, with a salad and baked potato, his usual fare. Lynn picked the fresh-caught trout with au gratin potatoes and oven-roasted asparagus. The waiter placed a basket piled with sourdough bread hot from the oven and a small platter with green onions, radishes, carrots, celery, and a creamy dip in front of them.

"Well, there goes the grocery budget for the month," Jake murmured, and Lynn chuckled.

Then she sobered. "I do hope this was worth it," she said.

"Oh, I think it is," Jake responded immediately. "See, there's Jeremy Walsh with his court and Ruth hunkering over in a corner watching enviously. We know the others from the Sugar Shack. And this is where Winnie came to ferret out who killed Jerianne. Obviously, she came to the right place."

Lynn agreed. "And possibly found the right person…or the wrong one."

Jake pulled a spare napkin close to him and found a pen in his shirt pocket. "So, who all do we have here tonight?"

Lynn shot a quick glance toward the noisy table. "I think the guy in the gray shirt is Kevin… something."

Jake wrote the name down and tapped his lips with the pen. "I believe he works for one of the construction companies. So, not that regular a Sugar Shack customer, and, let's see, I'm thinking his last name is Montgomery."

He wrote the last name followed by a question mark.

"The man in the red polo shirt with his back to us is Paul Davidson, an insurance salesman," Lynn added. "He's a Sugar Shack connection."

Jake added that name to the list and replied, "And the dark-haired woman in the white dress is Lucinda McDonnell. She's a realtor with one of the agencies in Red Lodge whose territory includes Cooke City."

Lynn looked again. "There's a guy at the bar next to the table who is joining in on the conversation, and he has a date or wife with him."

Jake leaned back in. his chair and stretched, using the motion to study the tabloid at the bar.

"He looks familiar, and so does she," he said.

Lynn nodded. "Yes, but not from the Sugar Shack."

"And not from Cooke City, either, "Jake replied as he made a note with two question marks on the napkin.

The waiter approached their table, bending down to ask if they needed anything and to tell them their dinners would be coming soon. Jake casually covered the napkin, but before the waiter could leave, he stopped him.

"It's our first time here," Jake began. "I see food being served in the bar area as well as here in the dining room. Is it the same menu?"

The waiter shook his head. "No, the bar menu features typical bar food like onion rings, sliders, burgers, fancy fries, potato skins, and other appetizer-type items," he responded.

Jake shook his head. "Wow, and do you wait on the tables in the bar as well as down here?"

"Most of the time, we don't unless we are short-staffed, like now," he replied. "Then we each have a table or two we cover in the bar as well as here."

Jake continued, "So you all sort of cover everyone? How are the tips?"

The waiter grinned. "Tips are good but they're better down here on the dining level… with some notable exceptions," he confirmed as his eyes drifted in the direction of Jeremy's table.

Lynn smiled up at him and said softly, "We heard about one of your waitresses being murdered. I'm so sorry that happened."

The waiter's expression sobered. "Yeah, I miss Jerianne. She was great, good with the customers, and always did more than her share. She was fun to work with."

A waving arm at a nearby table caught the waiter's attention and without another word, he rushed over to see what the diner at the table wanted. Lynn sighed.

Jake tapped the tabletop impatiently with his pen. "We have a lot of new information, but none of it points to any one person. It could be someone at the Walsh table or anyone else working here who knew Jerrianne."

Lynn agreed with his assessment.

"So, do we tell Palmer what we've uncovered?"

Lynn shook her head. "Not yet. This could all be totally innocent, and the murderer could be anyone else in town."

Jake agreed. "Still, Jeremy and his buddy Chad what's-his-name, with a construction contractor, insurance agent, realtor and a couple who look fairly well-heeled. That almost suggests something."

Lynn thought for a moment as she finished cleaning her plate.

"You're right… almost like a meeting. I wonder if…?"

"What?" Jake prodded as she hesitated.

"Well, it almost seems like someone is planning a new home."

Jake's eyebrows rose. "It does, at that. Now I'm convinced there's more to this mystery than we know so far."

CHAPTER 9

Slowly, painfully, deliberately, Winnie set one foot after another. One more step. Watch for treacherous ruts, loose rocks, and soft spots. She was terrified she would fall and not be able to get back up again. Her head pounded, and the sun's heat beating relentlessly on it didn't help. Worse, she had no concept of how far she had walked, and the sun was close to setting. It would be cold soon, when night fell on the mountains. Winnie knew from experience how swiftly the air cooled, how chill it would become.

"Keep moving," she warned herself. "Don't stop. One foot after the other. Ignore how thirsty and hungry you are. That will keep you safe until you are home."

So intent was she on staying upright and in motion, she didn't hear the sound of an approaching vehicle until it was nearly upon her.

Relief and hope of rescue were her first thoughts. But then, who would be driving up here with night coming? It wasn't the right time of day for campers to be traveling in this part of the wilderness, too close to nightfall.

"Oh, God, what if it's the person who hit me?" she gasped. "What if he or she has come back to make sure they finished me off!"

And with that horrible thought, Winnie lunged off the edge of the rutted road and staggered across a rock-strewn flat area rough with scrub brush. She hunkered down behind a line of boulders and held her breath, hoping whoever it was hadn't seen the movement. The vehicle was going slowly up the narrow roadway, dust floating up from its wake. The driver didn't slow down at all.

"Damn!" Winnie grunted. "It's a county sheriff's squad!"

She stood up to try waving down the vehicle. Just as she cried out, she heard a sound that struck terror through her whole body: the rattle of a snake. Carefully, Winnie turned her head to her right. On a flat surface of one of the boulders, barely two feet from her head lay a huge coiled-up rattlesnake. Worse, it was poised to strike. Without hesitation, Winnie threw her whole body sidewise to the left. Her foot caught on a dip in the rough surface, and she flew through the air down a slight decline, landing on her back. Her already injured head struck a rock. Bright stars bloomed across her vision, followed by darkness.

Detective Palmer stood outside his cruiser, studying the campsite area carefully. Eagle's Roost wasn't known to a lot of locals, much less tourists. It was on barely more than a whim that he had decided to drive up and see if anyone had been around the site. Just another place to look for the missing woman, but now that he was there, little hints that someone else had also been there recently stood out.

Palmer leaned against the squad's passenger door and studied the area intently. He noticed tire tracks that appeared to be fairly recent, still sharp and clear. He walked carefully over to a flattened-out spot next to the usual parking spaces and knelt down. He put his hand on the smooth sand and reached out to touch a piece of dried brush that was broken off. From there, he could see a line of jagged drag marks that looked like toe drags, as though someone had crawled over to a tree. From there, he followed shadowy footmarks and poked holes in the sand that led to a break in the rocky base of the cliff where a tiny stream splashed water into a natural basin.

"Hmmmm," he murmured, standing upright and looking back toward the road's egress.

It would have been helpful if whoever had been there within the past day or so had left some obvious sign, but he couldn't see anything that made him feel confident that he might have found where Winnie Fredricks had been. And so, he was going on instinct and a strong hunch when he strode back to his squad and radioed for assistance. It was getting dark fast, and the temperature was dropping. Not optimal conditions for a search, but Palmer was reluctant to wait until morning. If Fredricks was injured, as the clues seemed to indicate, waiting really wasn't an option.

It took nearly an hour for two other squads to join him.

"I believe she was here," he told the four deputies who joined him at the Eagle's Roost summit. He led them to a relatively smooth area at the head of the road. "You can just see small footprints and the marks of a walking stick. I think she started down the road, but if she is injured, she may have fallen."

Pulling strong searchlights from their trunks, the men began working their way down the road, one walking on each side of the road while Palmer and two others drove the squads slowly behind them, offering more light from their high-beam headlights and spotlights. It was tedious work in the deepening dark of the night. For more than two hours, they inched down the road, making wide sweeps with their powerful lights.

"FOUND HER!"

One of the men leaped off the edge of the roadway and sprinted across a short stretch of flat, brushy sand. Lying on her back with her head twisted up against a sizeable rock, Winnie looked small, old, and vulnerable. Palmer's heart was beating fiercely as he knelt beside her and felt for a pulse.

"Weak, but she's alive," he said, relief obvious in his soft voice.

Looking around, he realized that there just might be enough room to set a helicopter down.

"Jackson, get warmup blankets from the trunk," he ordered. "Morse, call into Red Lodge for the medi-vac copter, radio the coordinates."

While the men followed his orders briskly, Palmer and one of the other officers gently moved Winnie into a more comfortable position. She did not respond, which worried him greatly.

"Hang in there, old girl," he whispered.

Lynn was opening up shop the next morning at 8 a.m., juggling a large box lined with pink bags and expecting to see Ruth coming down the sidewalk at any moment. What she didn't expect was Detective Palmer's squad pulling up in front of the Sweet Shop. Lynn tensed as the big officer slid out from behind the wheel of his squad. Then she saw the smile on his face, and relief flooded through her.

Grinning widely, Palmer joined her at the doorway and said, "Let's talk inside."

Lynn finished unlocking the door and opened it. At the checkout counter, with her purse stowed away and a box of freshly made huckleberry-flavored saltwater taffy in the Sweet Shop's distinctive sacks perched on top of the counter, Lynn turned to Palmer with hope in her eyes.

"We found Winnie Fredricks late last night," Palmer said, wasting no time getting to the good news. "She was high on the Eagle's Roost road and apparently making her way back down."

Lynn gaped. "What on earth?"

Palmer held up a hand. "We believe that she was abducted, struck hard on the back of the head, and dumped up at the Roost, possibly left for dead. She recovered enough to start hiking back down, but somehow, she got off the road and fell, striking her head again."

Lynn took a deep, wavering breath. "How is she? Where is she?"

Palmer replied, "We were able to summon a medi-vac copter, and she was air-lifted down to Red Lodge for treatment. She has a severe concussion and is also suffering from exposure, mild dehydration as well as a few bumps and bruises."

"Oh, thank God!" she said, slumping against the counter.

Just then, Ruth came into the shop and stopped short when she saw Palmer. Lynn waved her over.

"Great news," Lynn told Ruth. "Winnie is alive and being treated down in Red Lodge."

Ruth's face lit up. "That's great news! Was she able to tell them what happened?"

Palmer answered, "Not yet. She was unconscious when we found her and has remained unresponsive so far today. With a concussion, it may take time to stabilize her. We are hopeful she will feel well enough to talk to us later today."

"Wow," Ruth replied, turning toward the open sliding doors into the Sugar Shack. "Is it okay if I tell Connie?"

Palmer nodded. "I don't see any reason not to," he said.

Lynn and Palmer watched as Ruth rushed across the shop floor and through the double doors into the Sugar Shack, where many of the town's regulars were already slurping down coffee and scarfing up donuts. Seconds later, they both heard the loud cheer as Ruth passed along the good news.

Palmer turned to Lynn with a somber look on his face. "That should get the ball rolling," he murmured.

Lynn nodded. "Yup, I'm betting the entire Cooke City population will know in less than two hours."

Palmer snorted a laugh. "Including someone for whom this will not be good news, I'm betting."

Lynn sighed. "I suspect you are right there."

Palmer gazed reflectively across the shop and into the Sugar Shack.

"What can you tell me about Ruth?" he asked.

Startled, Lynn stared at him for a moment before answering. "Ruth Greggory is from Gardiner originally, and moved here several years ago. She has worked for us for more than three years. Ruth is reliable, never misses work. In fact, I suspect she would have to be on her deathbed before she would call in sick."

Palmer gazed into the Sugar Shack for another long moment, then turned to Lynn.

"So, while your clerk is busy, I have a few questions," he murmured.

"Starting with, the county coroner will be releasing Ms. Baker's body in a few days. And so far, we have not been able to locate next of kin. We don't know who to release the body to for burial," Palmer said.

Lynn sighed sadly. "You can release her to us, Jake and me. I'll ask the community to help with a funeral."

Palmer replied, "Thank you. And I'm hoping you can give me a few leads. Did Ms. Baker ever mention anyone, family or friends, that you recall?"

Lynn thought for a moment and shook her head. "No, Jerianne never spoke about family. Not even an ex-boyfriend nor her husband."

Palmer responded, "I was afraid of that. She is not on any social media that we can trace except book promotions. Her bank account has no listed inheritors, and we have not been able to track any investments so far. It's as if she doesn't exist."

Lynn thought for a moment. "How about her publishers? Jerianne has published several books, both fiction and nonfiction. Hold on a moment."

Lynn left Palmer standing at the service desk while she went into the office and returned with one of Jerianne's books. Thumbing through the front and back of the book, she finally closed it with a snap.

"Odd, I didn't notice this before. There's no author's photo either on the front or back cover," she commented. "Here's her bio. Hmmmm, it says she has written seven books and countless magazine articles and has traveled extensively. No mention of where she lives or even where she is from. That's unusual. So, do you think she was in the witness protection program?"

Palmer shook his head. "When we couldn't trace her, we contacted the FBI. She's not one of theirs, or so they say, and there's not really that many in the program so it's doubtful they lost track of her."

Lynn pondered that news for a moment. "So, what we seem to have is her moving to Cooke City and becoming a ghost. I have to wonder why. What kind of experience would cause a woman to go into such deep hiding."

Palmer concurred. "Still, if she were afraid of someone, wouldn't she have recognized that person if they suddenly showed up here? It's a puzzle, but it doesn't solve the original mystery of why she was so brutally murdered. It was a crime of passion, not something a passing tourist would commit."

Lynn agreed. "So we are back to the suspect being someone here in Cooke City, not an outsider, which supports the attack on Winnie."

Palmer nodded and added, "Which brings me to my next request. Is there someone who can take Ms. Fredricks in after she is released from the hospital? She needs protection from whoever failed to kill her the first time. I suspect she was left up on Eagle's Roost to try to walk down and die as the result of a fall or the blow to her head. Whoever did this tried to make it look like a hiking accident of some sort."

Lynn answered, "Jake and I can watch over Winnie. But I hesitate to ask anyone else for help. I'm afraid someone we know is to blame."

Palmer nodded. "I'm afraid you're right."

CHAPTER 10

After Palmer left, Lynn called Jake and filled him in on what she had learned. After a long pause, Jake agreed that they could provide protective housing for Winnie.

"She can stay at our house in the mornings, and when I come to work in the afternoon, she can stay at the shop, and you can go home with her to take care of her cat and anything else that needs doing. Or her neighbor may be willing to be with her during the day," Jake said. "She can stay in our guest bedroom at night. I'm hoping we can get this resolved quickly, but I believe that's not going to happen."

Lynn also believed it wouldn't. "That will work. Now, about the funeral for Jerianne…"

Jake interrupted, "Just go over to the Sugar Shack and ask. I'm certain it won't take a day or two before enough people volunteer to help. The church will probably offer to hold the services, and we can talk to the funeral home in Red Lodge to help make arrangements for the cemetery."

"Okay, I'll start right now since the whole gang is over in the Sugar Shack," Lynn replied. "Thanks, Jake."

Jake grunted. "You're welcome but… I'm worried. We're getting too involved, and someone here is dangerous. We need to stick close together. Don't go anywhere alone, Lynn, or allow Winnie to wander off, either."

Lynn chuckled, "So what if Winnie and I are accosted?"

Jake laughed out loud. "I pity the person who even attempts to harm the two of you together."

On that happier note, a grinning Lynn hung up and headed into the Sugar Shack to rustle up some help for a funeral. As Jake predicted, it took less than 20 minutes for Jerianne's funeral to be roughly planned. While Ruth went back into Sweet Stuff to cover, Lynn stayed and listened to the suggestions being made. Slowly, she became aware of Jeremy Walsh's thoughtful stare, an uncomfortable feeling tingling along her shoulders and neck.

But on closer study, she realized Jeremy wasn't really looking at her but seemed to be far away and in deep thought. For once, the effervescent Chad was silent. When everyone had volunteered to put the funeral together, Lynn wandered slowly back into her shop.

"Did they say when Winnie is being released?" Ruth asked.

Lynn shrugged. "Possibly tomorrow or the day after. She is still recovering from two severe head blows. They want to keep her basically immobilized, and you know how tough that would be."

Ruth grinned. "Yup," she replied. "Has she remembered anything from before she was found yet?"

Lynn shook her head. "No, that may take a while. Or maybe never happen."

Three tourists entered Sweet Stuff and interrupted their conversation. The shop settled into its normal summer pace. Ruth finished her shift and left minutes before Jake arrived.

"You were right," Lynn told him. "It took less than half an hour to plan out Jerianne's funeral, with everyone taking on a task. Funny, though, Jeremy Walsh didn't contribute any comments or volunteer, and his sidekick, Chad, was mostly silent as well."

Jake grunted. "Hmmm, not what I would have expected. Well, time will tell," is all he said.

While Lynn took care of customers, Jake began rearranging the shop's back wall. When he was finished, there was a large opening left in the middle. That finished, Jake went out to his SUV and returned with his latest project, a four-foot by wide by three-foot high piece that featured flowing woods of various textures and colors worked into what looked like a rugged abstract wilderness with a perfectly preserved bone-white elk horn embedded into the design. Polished pieces of moss agate that blended with the wood tones were scattered along the crevices carved out on either side and beneath the horn. Within the horn itself, Jake had infused melted silver into some of the seams, then sealed it to prevent tarnishing.

Jake brought a ladder out from the storeroom. Carefully, he lifted the new artwork and hung it in place.

"Oh, Jake, that is incredible," Lynn breathed.

Before she could say more, the chimes over the Sweet Stuff door rang and Jeremy Walsh stepped tentatively into the shop. Before he could close the door, Old Lucy, who had been napping outside, pushed passed him and slunk across the floor. She spotted Lynn behind the counter and slipped in behind her, lying down at her feet.

Jeremy stood watching this with a bemused look on his face. Then, his attention was caught by Jake's masterpiece, and his expression changed to one of astonished pleasure. Without taking his eyes off the artwork, he crossed the floor and stood next to Jake, who was still on the ladder.

For a long, silent space, Jeremy seemed to examine every inch of the spectacular art. He reached out and almost touched it, hesitated, and dropped his hand. Then he sighed.

"How much?'

"Eight thousand," Jake replied without hesitation.

Lynn's eyes widened. Jeremy didn't react.

"Consider it sold," he finally. "Would it be convenient for you to let it hang here until I have a place for it?"

Jake nodded. Another weighted silence ensued.

Jeremy sighed again. "I loved her. Jerianne," he murmured. "I asked her to marry me. She put me off, but I hoped… I bought land and made plans to build a home here for us. No more summer rentals. I wanted a lifetime with her…here."

Lynn dared ask, "And now?"

Jeremy turned his distant gaze upon her. "Now? I want to stay, and I will build the home. I want… need to be here. Oh, and I will be paying any costs for the funeral and burial that aren't covered by her community and friends."

Lynn drew a deep breath. "That's generous of you."

Jeremy shook his head. "No, it's not just the least I can do; it's sadly the only thing I can do for her now."

With one long last look at the art he had purchased, Jeremy left the shop without another word.

Jake descended from the ladder and put it away in the storeroom. Coming back out, he said, "Well, that explains the bar party at the Timberline," he commented. "A realtor, a contractor, an insurance agent, and I supposed that couple at the bar behind them were the people who sold him the land."

"And Chad… what's his name," Lynn added. "But it doesn't explain Ruth. And Ruth just asked me if Winnie had regained her memory yet. And when she was coming back to Cooke City."

Jake winced. "Damn it! I hate this," he exploded uncharacteristically.

"Me, too," Lynn responded softly. "Me, too."

CHAPTER 11

"Jake."

No answer.

"Jake, are you awake?"

Jake grunted softly. "I am now."

Lynn murmured, "Do you think Jeremy Walsh killed Jerianne?"

Jake rolled onto his back and gazed up at the darkened ceiling for a moment.

"I suppose it's possible," he said at last.

Lynn rolled onto her side and raised up on one elbow.

"But he said he loved her, and I believed him," Lynn responded.

Jake sighed deeply and turned his head in Lynn's direction. In the dark, it was difficult to see much more than her outline against the moonlit window.

"People do kill people they think they love," he replied.

"Why? Jealousy? Anger? Rejection? If you truly love someone, wouldn't you want them to be happy no matter how it hurt you?" Lynn declared, her voice pensive.

"I would, and I know you would, but not everyone is like us," Jake pointed out.

Lynn flopped back on her pillow and lay there for a long moment.

"Jake, why do you suppose Jerianne was hiding here?"

Jake said, "What makes you think she was hiding?"

Lynn answered, "Palmer said they have been trying to trace her and haven't found out much. And the dust jackets on her books have no photos nor do they say where she lived, what her personal history was. Just a list of books she has published in the same genre. And he can't find any family, either. Even her publishers don't have additional information."

Jake grunted, "Or won't say. A privacy clause might even be part of any contract she signed."

"Humph, and what about Chad... what's-his-name? Why can't I ever remember his name?"

Jake chuckled. "I think it's something like Turner, but I'm not sure. He is annoying."

Lynn barked a short laugh. "He certainly loves annoying Jeremy."

"That's not all Chad loves," Jake quipped.

"Do you think Jeremy likes Chad?"

Jake laughed. "No, and that may be why Chad what's-his-name is so annoyed."

"Do you think Ruth does?"

"Does what?"

"Loves Jeremy?"

Jake started. "Now, that's something I hadn't considered. And it might explain a few things."

Lynn sighed. "Now we're back to the same conclusion... that someone who lives in Cooke City killed Jerianne and attacked Winnie."

"True," Jake replied. "Unless someone from Jerianne's past finally caught up with her. How likely is that?"

"Or," Lynn countered, "how likely is it that someone living here besides Jeremy or Chad or Ruth killed Jerianne? We're missing something."

Jake agreed.

"Are we going to get any sleep tonight?" Lynn murmured.

Jake sighed. "That's not likely, either."

Morning dawned bright, but Lynn felt anything but bright. Cupping a mug of coffee in both hands, she stared at the laptop screen in Sweet Stuff's back office. With the overnight orders handled, she wondered if Ruth would notice if she spent extra time researching and why that should worry her.

When the front doorbells jangled, and she could hear Ruth helping a couple of tourists, she keyed Jeremy Walsh's name into the search engine and waited while it summoned up whatever information it could find. What emerged was gratifying and surprising. It took Lynn only a few clicks to determine which Jeremy Walsh was the one she wanted to know more about. A few posted photos confirmed it.

Pulling a notepad close, she scanned through the reference files and quickly learned that Jeremy was a former attorney who had served for nearly two decades as a district attorney in the Chicago area. He had "retired" after one horrendous murder case conviction was overturned because of what the source described as bungled evidence. In the aftermath, Jeremy walked away from an eight-year marriage that had produced no children. Media sources described it as a total burnout.

"Hmmmm," Lynn murmured to herself. "That was six years ago. He seems to have moved about quite a bit, but the media lost track, and therefore lost interest, in him. He obviously isn't hurting for money."

Lynn completed her notes on Jeremy by listing that he had rented summer space the year before and that this was his second year of coming to Cooke City. She wondered if Jeremy came back because of Jerianne or for some other compelling reason.

"Enough for now," Lynn told herself as she shut down the laptop.

Taking a list of orders, she emerged from the stock room just as Ruth was coming into it. Behind her, Old Lucy was hesitantly walking but came to an abrupt halt and sat down when she saw Lynn. She almost seemed to grin while her bushy tail smacked down on the floor.

"How did Old Lucy get in?"

Ruth grinned. "She slipped in when the last two customers went out. Gave them quite a start."

Lynn grinned back. "I'll bet."

Checking her order list, Lynn began gathering items to pack for shipping. As she moved through the store, she glanced into the Sugar Shack. Sure enough, the whole gang was there this morning, including Jeremy and Chad. Turning, Lynn nearly tripped over Old Lucy, who jumped back and whined.

"What's the matter, old girl?" Lynn whispered. "Is someone in there that you don't like the looks… or smell… of? I wonder."

Old Lucy gazed up at Lynn as if she wanted to answer but couldn't think of a way. Lynn reached down slowly and rubbed the dog's head gently. Old Lucy sighed in contentment.

Jake arrived at the shop minutes after Ruth signed out for the day. He unboxed a few new elkhorn and wood sculptures and found space on the wall shelves to display them. While he worked, Lynn caught him up on her search efforts.

"I had no problem finding a lot of info on Jeremy Walsh," Lynn told him. "He appears to be exactly what he is, a fairly wealthy former attorney who has chosen to retire after some controversy. But why would someone like that come here? Considering all the places he could have chosen…" she trailed off.

Jake shook his head. "Who knows? Perhaps he's been through here a long time ago or heard people talking about Cooke City. Or saw something on television. It might be a bit remote, but it does have its appeal."

Lynn chimed in, "And it's small enough that there's little chance anyone living here would know who he is… or care, for that matter. We do tend to mind our own business, with some notable exceptions."

Jake laughed. "Yes, and one of those exceptions is going to be here tomorrow if the hospital releases her. If she spends much of her days here with you in the shop, she's going to be in close proximity to those who could be suspects. I'm really not feeling comfortable about this at all."

Lynn studied him thoughtfully. "You're right," she finally allowed. "But we do have another possible advantage."

Jake frowned. "What's that?"

Lynn explained how Old Lucy had slipped into Sweet Stuff and had spent a part of the afternoon staying close beside her. Jake glanced over at the dog, who was dozing beneath the service counter.

"Maybe we should bring Mickie with us, too," he suggested.

Lynn laughed out loud. "Oh, my, I can just see this. You, me, Ruth, Winnie, and two dogs. There won't be room for customers if this keeps up. And how do you expect Mickie to add to this protection project?"

Jake snorted. "A lot of sound and fury. She would raise enough ruckus it would scare anyone away."

They were still chuckling when Connie finally was able to close the Sugar Shack after shooing the last of the regulars out of her front door.

"It's good to see you both in good spirits," she said as she came through the sliding doors, smiling. "So, Winnie will be home tomorrow, God willing. We can help keep an eye on her with you. She has a lot of good friends in this community and should be safe here."

Lynn and Jake exchanged a quick glance.

"Yeah," Lynn thought to herself. "As long as one of those friends hasn't turned into a dangerous enemy."

CHAPTER 12

Winnie Fredricks' arrival home in Cooke City was as dramatic as her departure. The county sheriff's department decided the ride by ambulance over the treacherous Beartooth Pass would be too hard on the older woman, so they authorized a medi-vac helicopter to bring her. Word got out fast, and her arrival was heralded by dozens of residents and more than a few curious tourists.

Landing in a hotel parking lot not far from Lynn's home, Winnie was escorted from the helicopter to Detective Palmer's waiting squad car and driven through the city to Sweet Stuff, where she was warmly welcomed not only by Lynn, Jake, and Ruth but also all the regulars from Sugar Shack.

Seated at a table in the restaurant portion of the building, Winnie lost no time regaling her friends and dining tourists with her harrowing tale of her hike down from the mountain, the close encounter with the rattlesnake and the timely arrival of Palmer and his deputies, which she only knew about from hearsay.

Grinning, Lynn commented to Jake that she wasn't sure if the story was being embroidered upon with each telling or if Winnie was remembering more of what happened.

Jake grinned back but then said soberly, "Probably a bit of both. One thing for sure, Winnie is going to become a Cooke City legend."

Lynn agreed. "She's already considered one of the town's colorful characters. I hope we can keep her safe."

Lynn added, "And us as well."

It turned out to be a busy day at Sweet Stuff, with Ruth staying past her usual 3 p.m. shift end and Connie keeping Sugar Shack open an hour later than her usual closing time. The last residents reluctantly shifted from the restaurant to the store, and Jake brewed several pots of coffee while they lingered. When the last one finally wandered out, Winnie gave a huge sigh of relief and settled into a comfortable chair at the back of the store that Jake had brought from home for her.

"I thought they'd never leave," she moaned.

"Winnie! Are you feeling okay?" Lynn exclaimed.

Winnie smiled weakly. "I'm okay, still a bit stiff, achy and tired. It was so hard keeping up a brave front and trying to make light of that ordeal. I didn't want them to see that I'm scared out of my wits."

Jake studied her for a moment. "You should be. And it's a good thing you are because that will help ensure you don't do anything careless."

Winnie nodded. "Yup, I agree with you 100 percent," she said. "I'm going to stick to you two like glue."

Three customers came in through the chiming door, and Lynn went to see if she could be of assistance. Jake's worried eyes followed her across the shop and then he turned to Winnie.

"Now, you listen here," he warned. "I'm counting on you to do nothing that will endanger either you or Lynn. Do you hear me?"

Winnie nodded. "Loud and clear," she replied. "You are preaching to the choir, Jake. I learned that lesson hard. Someone out there is a murderous SOB, and I'm not taking any more chances with whoever it is."

Jake nodded back. "So here's the deal. You will come home with us tonight after we take you to your home to get whatever you need for an extended stay and to take care of your cat. We have a guest room all set up on the main floor. Neither you nor Lynn will be left alone, ever. Where she goes, you go."

"Got it," Winnie agreed.

After they closed up Sweet Stuff at 8 p.m., Jake took Winnie and Lynn to Winnie's house in his jeep. It took more than an hour to pack Winnie's clothing and other necessities because the dainty Siamese cat, Miss Elsie, demanded attention constantly, and so, too, did the neighbors who dropped by to visit. While Jake and Lynn carried suitcases and bags out to the jeep, Winnie and her feline companion wandered about the house, making sure they had everything needed and talking to a constant stream of Cooke City residents.

Finally, with the jeep loaded, Winnie left instructions with her friend and neighbor, Julie Harper, on where she would be and how often she would be there to see to the cat.

"I just wish they'd find my purse and flip phone," Winnie commented as they backed out of the short driveway. "Did the detective say anything about it?"

Lynn turned around from her seat in the front and frowned. "No, Palmer didn't mention it at all."

Winnie sighed. "I supposed I'll have to replace everything that was in it, which actually wasn't all that much. But did they recover my keys? I'm pretty sure they were in my purse. I guess I'll have to change all the locks on the house as well."

Over his shoulder, Jake replied, "That's an excellent idea. And we can help you get a new phone as well. We all should be carrying our phones day and night."

Lynn asked, "Have you remembered anything about that night?"

Winnie was silent for a moment. "Some things. I remember thinking it would be a good idea to drive to Silver Gate and check out Timberline Inn, where Jerianne worked. I parked and went inside, where Jeremy Walsh and his gang were up in the bar area. They kept placing orders that would bring Jerianne up there and teasing Jeremy. One would order an appetizer, and when Jerianne brought the order, another would order something. They thought it was funny, but Jeremy was visibly uncomfortable."

Jake responded, "I can understand that. If Jeremy was honestly in love with Jerianne, they were making him look like a fool. And they probably weren't fooling Jerianne, either."

Lynn added, "Right, and then what happened?"

Winnie continued, "I had to use the restroom, so I got up and wove through a mob to get to the right hallway. I think… I'm not totally certain, but I think I heard someone say something in that crowd, but it's really fuzzy. I know I decided I'd had enough and walked back through the crowd to the front door. Outside, I vaguely remember walking toward my car. That's it."

They were all quiet for a few minutes. As Jake pulled into the drive and got out to start unloading, Lynn asked Winnie, "Do you remember if Ruth Greggory was there?"

Winnie frowned. "No, not really, but she definitely wasn't at the table with Jeremy and the others, and when I went to the restroom, I didn't really pay any attention to who was around me. And that's when I heard the comment I can't remember. In fact, I feel it was the main reason why I decided to leave right away."

Jake walked around the jeep and helped Winnie down. He said, "In other words, anyone from the table group or in the area around the hall could have followed you out, and probably no one else would have noticed."

"Right," Lynn chimed in. "They could have excused themselves for some reason and basically disappeared into the mob."

Old Lucy drifted in out of the shadows and gave Winnie a rude start.

"Wow! That dog… or should I say wolf… is scary silent. She seems to have adopted you two," Winnie gasped.

Jake chuckled. "Yes, she has, and she has her suspicions as well."

Lynn explained Old Lucy's behavior at Sweet Stuff, to which Winnie shook her head and looked amazed.

"Who would have thought?" she murmured. "And what about Mickie? Is she a guard dog, too?"

Lynn laughed. "Believe me, if anything moves anywhere around the house, we will know. Mickie is our burglar alarm."

Later, after a light supper and a bit of television, Lynn showed Winnie to the guest room. As she turned down the bed and made sure Winnie had everything she needed, she decided to bring up the subject they seemed to have been avoiding all day.

"You know, it's extremely unlikely that the person who murdered Jerianne and assaulted you is a stranger, right?

Winnie nodded solemnly. "Right. That's what's so awful and scary. It almost has to be someone we know. I thought about that a lot this morning in the Sugar Shack, wondering if one of the customers is a killer. I hate to think it, but what else can we do? And now, who can we trust?"

CHAPTER 13

Lynn and Winnie arrived at Sweet Stuff a few minutes after 8 a.m. to find it busier than usual, with Ruth rushed and flushed. After a few minutes of watching Ruth trying to cope, Winnie tentatively asked Lynn if she could help the shop's customers and relieve Ruth.

"I don't know why not," Lynn replied. "You probably know the stock almost as well as we do."

When a large group of customers from a bus tour came in, Winnie lost no time greeting them and pointing out the most popular items on the shelves. Lynn kept an eye on her while taking in money and bagging the things people bought.

At one point, she heard Winnie say, "Now you see these neat pink boxes of huckleberry taffy? These are unique to Sweet Stuff, made in the commercial kitchen next door at Sugar Shack by our owner, Lynn. You need to keep a sharp lookout when you tour through Yellowstone because anywhere you see clusters of cars and tourists with cameras in hand blocking the road, it's a good bet there's a large bush of huckleberries close by with a bear in there!"

Some of the tourists gasped while the others grinned. But sales on the tasty taffy were brisk, as were huckleberry scented candles that Winnie assured the shoppers were hand-poured by Lynn in her studio. When the crowd dwindled down to a few shoppers left, Ruth joined Lynn to help bag the buys.

"Look at her go," Ruth said with a grin.

Lynn laughed. "Yup, I believe she missed her calling. What did she do, anyway?"

Ruth replied, "I think she was a grade school teacher."

"Humph," Lynn responded. "It figures."

The chimes on the door jingled, signaling the last of the customers leaving. Winnie watched them go and strolled across the shop to join Lynn and Ruth.

"Whew! That's hard work," she commented.

With Cooke City in the high summer tourist season, the rest of the day was equally as busy. At 3 p.m., when the Sugar Shack had closed and Ruth had left, Jake arrived a bit early. The three sat down to freshly brewed coffee and raisin biscuits from the Sugar Shack. Shortly thereafter, Detective Palmer came in with a manilla envelope under his arm.

"Coffee?" Jake offered.

"Absolutely."

"How about a raisin biscuit?" Lynn added.

"Absolutely."

"That bad?" Winnie queried.

"Absolutely."

That brought smiles and then laughter all around. They sipped and munched contentedly for a while before Palmer glanced around and got down to business. Lynn realized that the detective had probably waited until things had quieted down before coming in, which meant he had something serious to discuss.

"Okay," he said as he pulled two sheets of paper from the envelope. "Ms. Fredricks, I want you to look at some photos and tell me if you recognize any of these items."

Winnie glanced down at the top sheet. "That looks a lot like my flip phone," she replied. "And this one is almost definitely my purse."

The flip phone looked like so many others, but the purse was unique. It was a brightly colored, quilt-patterned fabric bag with carved wooden handles that was bought in one of Cooke City's specialty shops.

"Where did you find them," Lynn wanted to know.

Palmer hesitated. "Okay, they were in a plastic bag lying on the ground in the back of one of the hotels, next to the dumpster. It looked like the dumpster had been emptied, and the bag had apparently fallen off the side when the truck picked it up. One of the hotel employees found it when he took the garbage out from the hotel kitchen."

Lynn gasped. "That's a lucky break," she exclaimed.

Jake asked, "Any idea how long it had been in the dumpster?"

"Not long," Palmer said. "It was most likely on top and slipped off the side. The bag was in fairly good shape, not torn or particularly dirty."

Jake nodded. "Which seems to indicate that someone kept it for a while before discarding it."

"Right."

Winnie murmured, "What about the stuff inside?"

"We sent the bag and phone to the state lab in Helena," Palmer said. "They sent an inventory of items, including a wallet with some cash and credit cards inside. Also lipstick, gum, a couple of used hankies, a baggie of cough drops, a bottle of Tylenol, and a few other small things."

Winnie frowned. "But no keys?"

Palmer shook his head. "No keys."

"Hmmm," Winnie replied. "I have an extra set of car and house keys. And when I came home from Red Lodge, I went through the pockets of the clothing I was wearing to see if my keys were in any of the pockets. No such luck."

Lynn sighed. "We had better get the locks changed on your house, Winnie."

"I agree," Jake added.

And Palmer concurred. "Good idea, the sooner, the better."

"But what would anyone want from my house?" Winnie wondered.

"You," Lynn answered immediately. "You won't be safe until the person who did this is caught."

Winnie snorted. "Well, then, I guess you're stuck with me until then because I don't plan to be home alone again until he or she is. If necessary, I'll get a hotel room."

Jake grunted. "That won't be necessary, Winnie. We have no intention of leaving you unguarded."

Winnie smiled slyly. "Well then," she said again. "We don't need to change the locks, do we? And if someone does break in, that might give us some more clues as to who it is. Although I can't think of anything I might have at home that would make it a target."

Jake and Palmer exchanged looks.

"She does have a point," Palmer admitted, making Winnie's smile widen. "It might tempt someone. Just stay vigilant, please. And ask Winnie's neighbors to watch as well."

Jake laughed. "I don't imagine that will be necessary, but it will do."

CHAPTER 14

"Humph," Lynn grunted.

"What?" Jake asked.

From where she sat on the sofa with the laptop from Sweet Stuff propped on her lap, Lynn looked over and said, "I am trying to find more information on Jerianne, Ruth, and Chad… what's-his-name? Obviously, that last one is more challenging."

From her place in a nearby recliner, Winnie replied, "I believe Chad's last name is Chandler. I seem to recall someone mentioning that, but I can't remember who or when. Sounds theatrical, doesn't it?"

Lynn sighed. "Yes, it does. Please don't tell me every one of the potential suspects is not who they seem to be. I feel like Pandora opening that dratted box."

No one commented. Lynn sighed again and began keying search words into the laptop.

"Okay, so Chad Chandler may have a Facebook page. I'm finding several persons listed with that name, so now, if I can only narrow it down to the right one…. And bingo."

Jake and Winnie gazed expectantly across the room at Lynn. They could see her scrolling down the laptop's screen with an expression that went from quizzical to flabbergasted.

"Oh, my," she murmured.

"Yes," Winnie prompted.

At Lynn's continued silence, Jake and Winnie got up from their respective chairs and walked across the room to sit on either side of her. Winnie gasped, and Jake winced.

"Well, this is certainly … illuminating," Lynn finally commented.

If the series of posts available to nonfriends was any measure, Chad Chandler led a highly active and flamboyant second life online.

"I wondered," Winnie finally said.

Jake shook his head. "I suspected, too," he added. "But he is subdued in his behavior here as compared to what I'm seeing online. I wonder if Jeremy Walsh knows."

Lynn replied, "Oh, I'm sure he does. Jeremy doesn't strike me as naïve. I believe Jeremy tolerates Chad because he's witty and amusing up to a point, and I've seen Jeremy show signs that Chad has crossed the line a few times."

After several moments of scanning, Lynn shut down the site. Winnie sat back and studied the ceiling before commenting.

"That does make Chad a viable suspect," she stated. "If Chad is in love with Jeremy, he could have considered Jerianne a rival."

Lynn nodded. "Especially if he had learned Jeremy had asked Jerianne to marry him."

Winnie started and turned to look at Lynn. "What? I didn't know that."

Jake replied, "Jeremy said as much the other day. And I agree that information could have intensified the emotional atmosphere around that group Jeremy hangs out with."

"If Jerianne had said yes…" Lynn started.

"And Chad found out about it…" Winnie added.

"Then the situation may have reached a boiling point," Jake finished.

The three of them looked at each other and burst out laughing.

"Why do I feel as if I'm in an Agatha Christy novel," Winnie gasped out.

When the merriment died down, Lynn said, "Okay, let's try Ruth."

She keyed Ruth's name into the search engine with disappointing results; a lot of Ruth Greggorys, too many to go through individually. Lynn added Cooke City to the search line with no success.

"Try Gardiner instead of Cooke City," Jake suggested. "That's where I heard she was from."

Lynn tried that with a bit more success.

"Okay, she isn't on Facebook, but she is on Twitter/X," Lynn said. "Hmmm, and there's some newspaper articles referencing her from 12 years ago, before she moved to Cooke City. Wow!"

Jake and Winnie crowded close and read as Lynn scrolled down through the first article posted.

SEARCH FOR LOCAL MISSING TEEN CONTINUES

GARDINER MT _ The search for 17-year-old Anne Marie Greggory continues after she was reported missing last week, bringing hundreds of residents and volunteers from across the state to help in the search.

Last Friday, April 14, Greggory reportedly left school with two classmates, stopped in at a local restaurant for an hour, and then, after leaving them to walk home, disappeared. At about 7 p.m., her sister Gloria Ruth Greggory, 22, called Gardiner police to report her missing. The sisters' parents were out of town on business at the time.

The article went on in detail to describe the efforts to find Anne Marie and a few more bits of information. Scanning down, Lynn found several follow-up stories that grew smaller as no sign of the missing teen or new information became available. Then, a stark headline announced what Lynn feared.

BODY OF GARDINER TEEN FOUND IN PARK

GARDINER MT _ The body of 17-year-old Anne Marie Greggory, who has been missing since April 14, has been found in a remote area of Yellowstone National Park's southeast sector off a trailhead. Hikers found her remains beside a stream several yards off a trail and more than 5 miles from the nearest trailhead and roadway.

The grim discovery brings to a close an extensive three-month search conducted by Montana State Police and Yellowstone Park rangers, joined by hundreds of civilian volunteers. The teen was reported missing after she and two friends left high school and shared sodas at a local fast-food restaurant. When the teens split up, Greggory reportedly began walking home alone while the other two went in a different direction. Questioning had produced no witnesses who saw Greggory as she walked home nor anyone who may have been with her.

Greggory was reported missing later that evening by her older sister, Gloria Ruth Greggory, 22. Their parents were out of town on business and, after being contacted, returned home the next day.

An autopsy has been scheduled for Thursday. Until then, Montana State and local law enforcement are releasing no further information on how Greggory died and how she might have been transported so far from home. Funeral services are pending.

Lynn sighed. "How sad," she whispered.

"Do you think Ruth had anything to do with her sister's disappearance and death?" Winnie asked.

Jake said, "No, or at least not directly. Anne Marie would have gotten out of school around 3 p.m. and spent maybe an hour with her two friends. So, say they split up, and she started home around 4 p.m. Ruth reported that she was missing later that night. But, taking her or her body anywhere in Yellowstone's southeast region from Gardner would have taken hours. She wouldn't have had time."

"Unless…" Lynn hesitantly added. "Unless she locked her sister up somewhere or killed her sister and stashed the body somewhere. She could have reported her sister missing while she or her body was still in Gardiner."

Jake and Winnie were stunned.

"Oh, wow," Winnie finally exclaimed.

"That's pretty cold-hearted," Jake murmured.

Lynn continued, "Remember, it was mid-April, so not many hikers would likely have been out on the southeast trails. A person could have driven a vehicle down one of those trails if they knew the ground was frozen and the weather would hold. Some of them are wide and smooth enough."

"Oh, wow," Winnie repeated.

Jake added, "I wonder if Ruth was under suspicion at any time."

"Let's check the other articles," Lynn suggested.

Further reports were sketchy, with some implied conjecture that a person or persons unknown who were familiar with or lived in or near Gardiner might be involved. Since Ruth Greggory was not mentioned in any of the later stories, it seemed unlikely that she was ever considered a person of interest, as Lynn termed possible suspects.

Winnie sighed. "Now that I see these articles, I vaguely remember this case. I can't imagine why I didn't pay more attention at the time."

Jake answered, "Perhaps because it was halfway or more across the state, and besides a few locals who may have helped with the search, it didn't impact us much."

Lynn nodded, "And I sort of remember it mentioned, but when we came to Cooke City eight years ago, we avoided paying a lot of attention to the news. It's what we came here to escape. Now I wish I had."

They sat silently, staring at the laptop screen for several moments. Then Lynn stirred and shrugged.

"This brings up so many questions," she finally murmured.

"Like what?" Jake asked.

"So why did Ruth move to Cooke City? And why did she use her middle name to possibly deflect recognition?" Lynn mused.

"And why was she at the Timberline Inn, surveilling Jeremy's dinner party?" Jake added.

"What!?" Winnie exclaimed.

Jake explained, "After you disappeared from the parking lot in Silver Gate, we decided to have dinner at the Timberline Inn and check things out. Jeremy was at a bar table with a group of people, including Chad, Connie, Kevin Montgomery, Paul Davidson, Lucinda McDonald, and another couple."

Winnie stared at him. "Well, that's interesting."

"Why?" Lynn wanted to know.

Winnie answered, "Kevin Montgomery works for a construction company as a project manager, which means he covers a wide area, including Gardiner. And as an insurance agent based in Gardiner where he also lives, so does Paul Davidson. The same can be said of Lucinda, who is a realtor. Any one of them could easily have been in Gardiner the day Anne Marie disappeared."

Jake nodded. "Of course, and that means any one of them could potentially have been involved in Anne Marie's disappearance. From the photo, she was a lovely young woman."

Lynn agreed and added, "And that may have been why Ruth was watching them. Was Ruth there the night you went to the Timberline Inn?"

Winnie shook her head. "I don't believe so. I don't recall seeing her when I went to the restroom. Sadly, I don't remember seeing anyone yet. It all sort of fades out before I leave the restaurant."

Lynn closed the laptop and leaned back. "I wonder if Ruth suspects one of them was responsible for what happened to her sister and is trying to get some kind of evidence. If it's true and Jerianne's murderer also abducted and killed Anne Marie, then Ruth is in danger as well."

Winnie added, "And that leads to the next obvious question. Did Jerianne learn about the earlier murder and decided to work on a story about the cold case?"

The three sat in silence for a few moments.

Lynn finally commented, "And the next obvious question is, what do we do about this? Do we tell Detective Palmer?"

Jake shook his head. "Chances are, Palmer knows. He's been in county law enforcement at least that long, I'm guessing. And remember, Gardiner is a small community, less than 1,000 year-round residents. It's like Cooke City in that there's a limited pool of suspects."

And Lynn added, "Yes, and you know exactly what he will say if we do talk to him. First, he can't discuss the ongoing investigation, and second, he should stay out of it because it's too dangerous."

Winnie nodded vigorously. "I can attest to that."

Jake concluded, "I vote we quietly pursue whatever we can safely check on."

Lynn and Winnie reluctantly agreed.

CHAPTER 15

Lynn and Winnie were headed out of the door early the next morning when the phone rang. Lynn almost didn't answer it but had second thoughts. She didn't even get a chance to say "hello" before Ruth's voice burst through.

"Lynn, thank God! Someone broke into Sweet Stuff! Your laptop is missing," she yelled.

Lynn took a deep breath and said, "It's okay, Ruth. I took the laptop home because I didn't finish re-ordering stock yesterday."

But before she could continue, Ruth cut into her answer.

"But it's not the only thing… the back door was jimmied, and your desk was rifled through. Things were moved on the shelves, and some of the furniture was moved, too."

Lynn stared at Winnie, quite taken aback. "Did you call Detective Palmer?"

Ruth's almost breathless response was, "Yes! He's on his way. I didn't touch anything, and the Sugar Shack might have been tossed as well. The sliding doors were partially opened. I know you never leave them unlocked."

Lynn told Ruth that she and Winnie were on their way, then rushed into the workshop to let Jake know what was going on. Jake immediately set his latest project aside.

"I'm going with you," he stated. "Let's take the Jeep down."

In less than 10 minutes, they arrived at Sweet Stuff to find Ruth pacing up and down outside the front door and holding several customers at bay. Moments later, Palmer arrived as well, followed by a crime scene investigative team.

"Did Connie say anything about the Sugar Shack?" was Lynn's first question.

Ruth shook her head. "No, she didn't, and I don't understand why she didn't notice that the doors between us and her were open about a foot."

Winnie said, "Maybe she just didn't notice. She comes in through the back and starts on the morning's baking around 4 am with Sam. She may not have even come out from the kitchen."

"Hmmmm," Jake murmured. "I suppose that's possible."

Palmer approached them and asked, "Did any of you go inside the stock room?"

At Ruth's nod, he added, "Did you notice anything missing?"

"No, just moved around," Ruth said thoughtfully. "The desk looked as if it had been gone through. And I thought Lynn's laptop was missing but she took it home last night so it's safe. Also, the sliding doors between us and Sugar Shack were open, and we always leave them locked when we close up."

Palmer's eyebrows rose. "You may have lucked out with the laptop," he commented. "Do you leave money on the premises overnight?"

Jake replied, "Not much. I take the day's receipts to the bank dropoff around 7:30 pm or so, which leaves only half an hour's sales receipts, which are always locked in the safe."

Jake led Palmer back to the stock room and showed him where the safe was located behind one of the stock shelves. Things had obviously been moved, but it appeared the safe had not been broken into.

"To be on the safe side, so to speak, please open the safe," Palmer said. He waited while Jake opened the safe and examined its contents.

"Nothing appears to be missing or even sorted through," he responded.

"Okay, please stay outside for the time being," Palmer said.

They watched as he went through the sliding doors and back to the counter, where he sat down on a stool and began questioning Connie. A uniformed officer stood guard on the sliding doors to prevent any Sugar Shack customers from entering Sweet Stuff. After Connie's shocked reaction, she led Palmer into the rear of the restaurant where the kitchen, storage, and office were housed.

Ruth turned to Lynn and said, "Nothing appeared to be moved or missing in the store area."

Lynn nodded. "Someone was fishing for information."

Ruth looked shocked. "But why, for goodness sake."

Lynn hesitated, then said softly, "We know how you lost your sister. I'm afraid that perhaps the person who murdered Jerianne and abducted Winnie is trying to find out how much we know."

Winnie started. "Wait a minute, Lynn. What does Jerianne's murder have to do with what happened to Ruth's sister?"

Lynn sighed. "What if Jerianne came across the newspaper articles about Ruth's sister and decided to research for a novel? And what if she asked questions that let someone know she was digging into the past? The wrong someone."

Winnie groaned. "So now we have even viable motives for murder and kidnap," she murmured. "Nothing like complicating things. I thought it was jealousy."

Ruth looked sad and defeated. "I tried to keep that part of my past hidden because I wanted to find the person responsible for Anne Marie's death. That's why I moved to Cooke City, away from my parents, to protect them. Plus, the possible suspect might not remember or recognize me here, out of place, so to speak. It's been

12 years. At that time, we all were fairly sure it was a chance encounter that led to Anne Marie's death and not any ongoing relationship. There wouldn't likely be a reason for a stranger to remember his victim's sister after all these years."

Lynn was thoughtful for a moment. "Ruth, do you recall Jeremy Walsh ever being in Gardiner while you lived there? I mean, 12 years or more ago?"

Ruth immediately responded, "No, not at all. He only showed up in Cooke City a little more than a year ago. I recall he rented a cottage close to Silver Gate, where he probably met Jerianne working at the Timberline Inn. I believe that's why he came back this summer. I got the impression he doesn't tend to stay very long in any one place."

Jake joined the conversation, saying, "And what about Chad Chandler?"

Ruth grimaced. "Oh, him. He plays a wide field, but I feel that field has narrowed since he met Jeremy. And they met before Jeremy came here the first summer. That much was obvious. How Jeremy tolerates Chad is not so clear."

Palmer interrupted by opening Sweet Stuff's front door and saying they could come inside. About half a dozen customers followed Ruth, Lynn, Jake, and Winnie inside.

"Can I clean up the fingerprint powder and stuff," Ruth asked Palmer.

He grinned. "Yup. We're all done here."

Palmer took a few steps toward his cruiser, then paused and turned around to face them.

"I don't have to tell you not to investigate this on your own, do I?" he said sternly. "We may be dealing with a double murder and a brutal abduction. This person is dangerous."

Lynn started. It was clear that Palmer knew about Ruth's sister and had no trouble putting two and two together. The moment he left with the investigative crew, Connie rushed over from Sugar Shack, asking all kinds of questions. Lynn had a few of her own.

"Connie, didn't you see the sliding door was open?" was the first thing she asked.

"No, Sam and I had extra baking to do this morning for a huge order going to the church for Jerianne's funeral this afternoon," Connie explained. "We didn't come out of the kitchen until time to open, and Sam opened up."

"Did you find anything missing or moved around?" Winnie asked next.

Connie nodded. "Moved around, but nothing taken except some day-old banana nut muffins. Curious, that's all we are missing."

Lynn frowned. "Banana nut muffins? Which customers like those?"

Connie thought for a moment. "You know, there are a few customers who like them, especially one of them, but I can't remember who that is at the moment."

Lynn sighed again, and this time Winnie and Connie joined her. Jerianne's funeral was scheduled for 2 pm with an afternoon tea at the church before interment at the cemetery. Another rough spot to get through, Lynn thought. And they'd have to close Sweet Stuff to attend.

Standing behind the checkout counter, Lynn turned to Ruth and Winnie.

"So, do we heed Palmer's warning?" she asked, looking from one woman to the other. "Ruth, what's wrong?"

Ruth was staring at her with a stricken look, tears in her eyes. "I never told them," she whispered.

"Told them what?" Winnie demanded to know.

Ruth took a deep breath, looked around to see if anyone else was near, and then murmured, "Anne Marie came out to me a few months before she was… abducted. I promised to never tell anyone. It was her choice if and when to …"

Winnie's eyebrows rose. "You mean, your sister was gay?"

Ruth nodded miserably. "And all through that horrid investigation, I so wanted to say something, but my parents didn't know. How could I break my sister's confidence? What would they have said? Would they even have believed me? And I thought at the time, 'What difference would it make now.'"

Lynn gasped. "Oh, my, that certainly complicates things. Now, we really have broadened the field of potential suspects. Did you have any suspicions? Is that why you were watching that group around Jeremy?"

Ruth sighed deeply and said, "That group included Lucinda McDonald, the realtor who sold Jeremy his homesite. She was one of Anne Marie's classmates. In fact, she was one of the two who were with my sister at the restaurant just before she disappeared."

"Oh, my God," Winnie breathed. "You have to tell Palmer. You have to."

Lynn agreed. "Let's call and tell him right now. Ruth, it's been 12 years, and I'm sure you realize how important this information could be."

Ruth shook her head, a rueful expression on her face. "It's even worse than that. Anne Marie went to school with Paul Davidson's son. They still live in Gardiner. And so did Kevin Montgomery and his family at the time."

Lynn groaned. "That means everyone surrounding Jeremy can possibly be connected to Anne Marie's murder," she muttered.

Ruth reluctantly conceded that it was time to "come clean," as she put it to Lynn and Winnie. Jake, who had come into the front of the shop just in time to hear the last thing Lynn said, agreed wholeheartedly.

"Let's get this over with," Ruth finally muttered. "He's probably going to come back… I just hope this doesn't interfere with us getting to Jerianne's funeral."

CHAPTER 16

Jake locked up Sweet Stuff and hung a sign saying, "Back at 4 p.m." on the front door while Lynn, Winnie, and Ruth got into the Jeep. After a moment, Ruth commented, "Well, it was convenient that Palmer stayed in town for the funeral. And we don't have to have this discussion before it."

Lynn grinned, looking back over her shoulder to where Ruth and Winnie sat bunched up in the Jeep's cramped back seat.

"I should have guessed," she replied. "Don't the police always attend funerals to see who shows up?"

Jake laughed outright. "Right, but in this case, it's going to be the entire town anyway; no help there."

As it was, they could have more easily walked from Sweet Shop, what with all the cars lined up and parked along every road leading to the church. In one way, it was gratifying to Lynn to see so many people arriving. But then, she realized the likelihood that almost every business in town would be closed for at least the next few hours. Connie had closed early, too, sending all the regular customers on their way to the funeral.

"There's Connie going in now," Winnie pointed out. "We could join her if there's enough room. The church is going to be standing room only at this rate."

In the end, they were only able to find seats toward the rear of the church, sitting silent and absorbed by the number of people filing in and somberly taking seats.

"Who is that?"

Lynn glanced at Ruth and followed her finger point.

"I don't know, but she's going all the way to the front of the church, so she must be part of the family."

"What family?" Jake murmured.

All of them gazed at the young woman, tall with stylishly cut dark brown hair, dressed in black, who took a seat at the front left of the aisle, across from Jeremy Walsh and several of his friends who had commandeered the aisles usually reserved for family..

"She looks familiar," Ruth whispered.

Before anyone could comment, the church's minister stepped to the podium and the soft music that had been playing faded away.

"Dearly beloved, we are gathered today to say farewell to Jerianne Baker, a loved and respected member of the Cooke City community for several years. The manner of her death has left us all stunned and saddened. But in mourning her loss, let us not lose sight of the good times she spent with us…."

Lynn let the minister's words recede into the background as she looked around the crowded room.

"It's not so much who's here, but is there anyone missing?" she mused. "Would he or she be more conspicuous by their presence or absence? This isn't a police drama on TV or a mystery novel. Real people don't always do what you expect them to do."

When those attending rose to sing a hymn, Lynn was so deep in thought that Jake had to nudge her. When the music ended and the attendees sank back onto their pews, the strange woman in black rose and, with a calm, confident demeanor, took her place at the podium.

"Good afternoon, neighbors and friends of Jerianne Baker," she said in a soft, compelling voice. Allow me to introduce myself. I am Belinda Baker Randolph, Jerianne's sister."

Her words created a stir. Lynn stared at the woman with a faint smile. "Now we're going to finally get some answers," she thought.

With a sad smile, Belinda Baker Randolf looked out at the crowded church and began, "First, I want to thank each and every one of you for how you have come together to make this funeral possible. It shows not only how much you cared about my sister but also demonstrates the deep compassion and decency of the Cooke City community as a whole. So let me tell you about my little sister.

"I know from Jerianne how much you value personal privacy, and that was one of the reasons why Jerianne decided to stay in Cooke City. You see, she was married with two small children about six years ago. They were so happy and doing so well until tragedy struck. Her husband, Terry, and their two small children, Michael, who was five, and Linda, who was three, were killed in an auto accident.

"Jerianne was critically injured, and it took a long time for her to recover. After that, she felt she couldn't stay in our hometown with all the bittersweet memories. She moved first to one town, then another for almost three years. Through that time, she took several college-level writing classes and fulfilled her childhood dream of becoming an author. Finally, she discovered Cooke City. She was immediately struck by the way people accepted her without prying. She didn't want sympathy or pity. She simply wanted to get on with her life as best she could. Further, she didn't want her tragic life used to seel her books. Jerianne was an intensely private person who hoped her writing would stand on its own as valid.

"Soon, as her calls and emails indicated, she found not only acceptance without question but new friends. Those she worked with at the Sugar Shack and Timberline Inn were among them, as were many of you who were customers and neighbors. Her writing career was becoming more successful. She loved her little log cabin and especially her relationship with a singularly unusual dog… Old Lucy."

Belinda gazed down at the front row where Jeremy Walsh sat with a determinedly calm face.

"And for her, one new friendship held out the promise of a new love. I want to share with you, Jeremy, the strong feelings she had that you could help her move past her overwhelming sense of loss and fear. She told me just a few weeks ago that she was seriously considering your proposal of marriage and hoped to reach the point soon where saying 'yes' was possible."

Jeremy groaned out loud and began sobbing, his reserve broken. Chad grabbed a nearby box of tissues and shoved a wad of them into Jeremy's hands.

"I am truly sorry that things didn't work out that way. She deserved happiness. But someone took that away from her. And you."

Belinda raised her head, her expression grim. She scanned the crowd for a moment before continuing. "Someone here in Cooke City took this chance at happiness away from Jerianne and Jeremy. I cannot imagine what could have caused anyone to resort to murder and, most of all, kill my sweet sister. But now, I want to focus on you, and I invite you to share your personal experiences with Jerianne as we celebrate her life."

Belinda stepped down from the podium and the pastor resumed his place, inviting anyone in the audience to stand and contribute to the tribute to Jerianne.

As one after another of Cooke City's residents stood and shared their memories, some bringing tears and others gentle laughter, Lynn only half listened.

"How horrible to have survived an accident that killed her entire family and then come to this end," Lynn mused. It made Jerianne's death even more sad. She barely heard the pastor as he wrapped up the funeral with an invitation to join their fellow mourners in the church's fellowship hall for refreshments before the private burial. Only a few had received invitations to the cemetery, including Lynn and Jake. Ruth and Winnie were not among those chosen. Instead, they would reopen Sweet Stuff and hold down the fort until after the interment. Since the funeral ended slightly after 3 p.m., Connie wouldn't be reopening Sugar Shack that day.

During the reception, Belinda approached Lynn and Jake.

"I wanted to thank you for being such a good neighbor to Jerianne," she began. "Detective Palmer has asked me to go through the cabin in case there's something of significance he overlooked. Would it be all right if I visited you afterward?"

Jake replied, "Certainly, but we won't close Sweet Stuff until 8 p.m. if that works for you."

Belinda agreed that it would be no problem. With the fellowship hall slowly clearing, those chosen to attend the interment gathered at the front door while the rest wandered off to their respective homes or businesses.

CHAPTER 17

With Sweet Stuff closed for the night and a light supper finished, Lynn sat with Jake and Winnie on the wide wrap-around porch, watching as Detective Palmer waited for Belinda. Jerianne's sister was going through the cabin, choosing things to keep before going home. The three were mostly silent, each deep in their own thoughts. The sharp sound of Lynn's flip phone startled all three.

"Hello," Lynn responded, then handed the phone over to Winnie with a whispered, "it's Julie."

Winnie took the phone and said, "What? No, we stopped in this morning before opening Sweet Stuff to collect the mail and feed Miss Elsie. We haven't been back there since. Why?"

Jake and Lynn watched in concern as Winnie calmed Julie and asked, "What's different? Yes, I know, but… yes, I was in there. The medicine cabinet? That's not good… you don't have to call them. Detective Palmer is next door with Jerianne's sister. I'll tell him, and we'll be there pronto."

Jake was already standing up as she hit the off button.

"What happened?" Lynn asked.

Winnie frowned. "Julie thinks someone has been in my house. She went over to give Miss Elsie fresh water and put down some kibble. She said something didn't look right, so she went through the house. The medicine cabinet in the bathroom was open and cracked. I know it was closed when we were there this morning because I needed to bring refills for my pill sorter."

Jake nodded. "I'll tell Palmer. You get ready to go."

Jake trotted down the porch steps and across the lawn. Lynn and Winnie went into the house to grab jackets as the night was cooling down rapidly. When they returned outside, Jake was back on the porch, digging the jeep's keys out of his pocket.

"Palmer said I should follow him to Winnie's. Lynn, he asked if you could stay with Belinda while we're gone."

Lynn sighed but understood that there was no need for a crowd. They probably wouldn't be allowed into Winnie's house anyway. She watched as Jake and Winnie climbed into the jeep and waited until Palmer came out to his squad car. As they drove away, she crossed the lawn and approached Jerianne's cabin.

"Belinda!" Lynn called from outside the front door.

"Come in," Belinda answered. "I'm in the bedroom."

Lynn slowly walked into the living room area and crossed to the small hallway that led to the bathroom and bedroom. Inside, she found Belinda going through some of Jerianne's clothes. As she entered the small room, Belinda turned from the closet and sank down on the bed.

"I'm at a loss. I don't know what I'm supposed to do with all of Jerianne's things," she sighed. "She leased this cabin with most of the furnishings included. So, it's all the personal items that need to be sorted."

Lynn thought for a moment. "I supposed you could box them up and ship them home," she suggested. "That way, you don't have to go through them in a hurry."

Belinda nodded. "That's a great idea. I flew here, so there's not much I can carry home."

Lynn said, "I can help with that. How long did you plan on staying?"

"Another couple of days, but I left the plane ticket open-ended just in case."

Lynn sat down on a small, upholstered chair next to the bed and smiled. "I can bring boxes from the shop and other places and help you pack. I think Winnie wouldn't mind helping as well. It won't take us long with three working on it."

"I don't know how to thank you," Belinda replied. "I mean, I sort of feel like I know you even though we have never met in person before."

Lynn took a chance and asked, "I'm curious. How did Palmer find you?"

Belinda shook her head. "I found him. When Jerianne didn't call or text, I grew quite concerned. That wasn't like her at all. I finally gave up trying to reach her and called the sheriff's office to request a welfare check on her."

Lynn grinned. "I'll bet that came as a surprise to Palmer."

Belinda nodded with an answering smile. "I'm sure it did. He told me he had been searching for next of kin without success. Even the publisher wouldn't divulge any of Jerianne's personal information. And I'm not certain how much they knew. She couldn't bear for anyone to know what happened. Jerianne couldn't take the pity, the sympathy, the whispers … you know how some people are. That's why she loved Cooke City so much. Everyone minded their own business."

Lynn sighed. "And now we are prying into everything. This has made me realize how little we know about the people we see every day. Normally, it wouldn't be an issue, but now…"

Belinda agreed. "Now we need to know who was so threatened by what Jerianne knew that they killed her. And from what I've heard, attacked your friend Winnie."

Lynn said, "Why don't we go back to my house and have coffee while we wait for Jake, Winnie and Palmer? And I can start calling around about boxes for Jerianne's things."

Together, they left the cabin and walked across the lawn to the A-frame in the deepening night. In the kitchen, Lynn put on a pot of coffee and arranged the cookies she had in the cupboard on a plate. While the coffee brewed, she fed Mickie and refreshed her water bowl. They had just settled in the kitchen with steaming mugs when they heard cars pulling up in front.

Moments later, Jake called in from the front door, "We're back! Is that coffee I smell?"

Before Jake could close the door behind Palmer and Winnie, Old Lucy squeezed through and headed straight for the kitchen. Jake followed, grinning.

"Wow, I didn't even see her coming," he exclaimed as he trailed along behind her.

Old Lucy stopped abruptly just inside the kitchen area, causing Jake to bump into her. She focused sharply on Belinda, then slunk across the floor to stand in front of her.

Belinda gasped. "Is this Old Lucy? Oh, wow, she's huge!"

Belinda held out a hand tentatively toward the dog. Old Lucy reached out and touched it, then licked it gently. Stepping closer, the grizzled old dog sidled up to Belinda and laid her head on the woman's lap. She sighed deeply. Belinda blinked back tears.

"Jerianne teased me so much about how she had made friends with a wolf," she explained. "Of course, she knew Old Lucy wasn't a wolf... or was she? Maybe part wolf?"

Jake said, "No one knows for sure. Old Lucy has been around for years. We don't even know where she came from or if she ever had an owner. I suppose it's possible a female wolf mated with a dog, and Old Lucy was born in the wild."

Belinda added, "She's everything Jerianne said she is."

Palmer cleared his throat. "Okay, folks. Here's the deal. It appears someone used Mrs. Fredrick's keys to get into her home. Things went through, but the most worrisome thing was that the medicine cabinet was rifled. We bagged all the medications inside the cabinet and home just in case they had been tampered with."

Winnie sniffed. "Yeah, good thing I picked up a week's worth this morning. Now I have to get the prescriptions all refilled and buy new over-the-counter ones."

Lynn responded, "Yes, but it's better than taking a chance on those medications being tampered with."

Belinda added, "Someone is really afraid of what you might know. I'm so sorry you all have to go through this. It's awful."

"But not as awful as what happened to Jerianne and Winnie," Lynn said.

Palmer stated, "We are going to find whoever is responsible for this; the sooner, the better."

CHAPTER 18

After Palmer left to take Belinda to her hotel, Lynn, Winnie, and Jake settled in around the kitchen table. Mickie and Old Lucy curled up nearby, the latter on the rug by the back door.

Winnie heaved a long, mournful sigh, followed by what sounded suspiciously like a sob.

"What's wrong, Winnie," Lynn asked.

"I want to go home!"

Lynn nodded, and Jake grimaced.

"I mean I like being with you and feeling safe, but I hate this whole situation," Winnie continued. "I miss my cat. I miss going out every day and doing the things I love to do. I miss my neighbors… well, most of them. I want my life back."

Jake murmured, "So do we all."

Lynn glanced sharply at him before turning to Winnie. "I know you do, sweetie, but you need to be safe for the time being. No one is going to get to you with Jake and me here to protect you."

Winnie sniffed. "I know, I know. I just feel so useless and miserable. I wish we knew if the police were making any progress. Palmer doesn't say anything."

Jake responded, "He can't, it's an ongoing investigation."

"I know that, too. He certainly says it enough," Winnie grouched.

"I've got an idea," Lynn ventured. "How about we go to Sweet Stuff in the morning? Then, once Ruth is set for the day, we'll go over to your house. Maybe we can ask your neighbor, Julie, to stay with you for an hour or so while you spend time with Miss Elsie at home. I can come back, or Julie can walk you to the shop when you're ready to leave."

Winnie brightened visibly. "That sounds good, Lynn. You're such a good friend."

Jake added, "Okay, but make sure both of you are never alone."

Winnie was silent for a moment. Then she said, "You know, we sort of have an idea of who some of the suspects are. I mean, Ruth was watching them at the Timberline Inn. And we think it's all connected to the death of Ruth's sister. Couldn't we kind of investigate on our own?"

Jake frowned. "What do you mean, exactly?"

"Well, what about alibis for the time of the murder?" Winnie answered.

Lynn gasped. "Surely you don't think we can ask them?"

Winnie shook her head vigorously. "No, not at all. But it might be possible to ask other people where they were. Like, if we talked to some of the wait staff at the Timberline Inn about the night Jerianne was killed. Were Jeremy, Chad, and the rest all there like they seem to be almost every night? Was anyone not there?"

Lynn thought for a moment. "Well, that was on a Sunday night, apparently around 10 p.m. or later. Jerianne must have come home right after the dining room services ended. The bar would have been open until 2 a.m."

Winnie nodded. "So, if the whole gang was there after she left, the questions would be for how long and did anyone leave early."

Jake looked from Winnie to Lynn and back. "If you are suggesting we go there for dinner, I decline. That was far most expensive than it's worth."

Winnie grinned. "Noooo, I thought we'd just wander over there for a drinky-poo or two."

Lynn laughed out loud. "Oh, lord, Winnie…"

Winnie smirked. "And while we're at it, how much do we actually know about them? I know we found out that Jeremy is a retired lawyer. Chad is… something else. But what about Paul Davidson or Kevin Montgomery."

Jake said, "Paul Davidson is an insurance salesman. I think he covers a fairly large area, including Gardiner, where he lives with his wife, plus Red Lodge and some other communities."

Lynn added, "And Kevin is a building contractor with pretty much the same size territory, except I thought I heard he lives in Red Lodge now."

Winnie chimed in, "And what about Lucinda McDonald? As a realtor, she probably covers roughly the same area as well. Doesn't she live in Gardiner?"

"I'm not sure," Lynn said. "I think her home office is in Gardiner but I'm not certain of where she lives. Or, where any of them lived 12 years ago when Anne Marie died."

Jake grunted.

"What?" Lynn wanted to know.

"And we're doing this… why?" Jake asked.

Winnie replied, "Because inquiring minds want to know. Besides," she added, gently patting the back of her head, "I have a vested interest in whoever bopped me over the head and tried to kill me."

Lynn shook her head. "There's that."

Jake leaned back in his chair and studied to two women across the table from him. "Okay, we do this but… we do it in a way that ensures we are all safe or we don't do it at all. Understood?"

"Understood," both Lynn and Winnie said in unison.

The next morning, Lynn and Winnie opened Sweet Stuff at 8 a.m. Ruth arrived on their heels. Once the shop was up and going, Lynn walked Winnie to her home several blocks away. After a quick visit with Winnie's next-door neighbor, Julie Harper, Lynn was delighted to see Winnie settle happily in with a pot of her favorite tea, plus Miss Elsie and Julie for company before she returned to work.

"So, how is that going to work out," Ruth wanted to know.

"It's looking good," Lynn replied. "Winnie was really out of sorts last night, miserable and homesick."

Ruth nodded. "I can't blame her. I would absolutely hate to have my whole life disrupted like that. It must feel great to get back to some sense of normalcy."

Lynn didn't answer for a moment. Instead, she was distracted by the noise and bustle of the Sugar Shack. With the sliding glass doors open, it seemed louder than usual.

"You know, Ruth, I have never really paid much attention to who all comes and goes at the Sugar Shack," Lynn murmured. "I mean, look at the customers. So many are locals. There's Jeremy and Chad at that table in the corner, and Paul Davidson is at the counter seats. Is this normal?"

Ruth responded, "It didn't used to be, but I think in the past two to three months, it seems Jeremy and his entourage have been coming in more regularly. It may have had something to do with the thing Jeremy had about Jerianne."

"Thing?"

"Yeah," Ruth said, "At first, Jerianne didn't want anything to do with Jeremy. I remember overhearing Chad make some rude remark and Jeremy responding with, 'She's particular.' Mostly, I think he hung out at the Timberline Inn at night mostly to be around Jerianne. That was last summer when he and Chad were here. But this year, he has been coming into the Sugar Shack in the mornings. That must have started about the time he returned to Cooke City fpr the second summer."

"Hmmmm," Lynn said. "But Paul isn't sitting with them."

Ruth explained, "Sometimes he does, and other times he sits at the counter and talks to Connie."

"And what about that building contractor, Kevin Montgomery?"

Ruth thought for a moment. "I don't see him here all that often, but he's really busy this time of year. We have such a short summer that the outdoor jobs pile up fast."

Before they could continue the discussion, a busload of tourists pulled up in front, and dozens of shoppers descended on the Sugar Shack and Sweet Stuff. The ensuing crowd kept them busy for more than an hour while the tourists bought bags of baked goodies and every sort of Western souvenir to take on the next leg of their excursion.

"Whew," Ruth breathed. "That's going to make for a good bottom line today."

"It sure is."

"And I'm wondering why you are so curious about Jeremy and his cronies," Ruth murmured.

Lynn hesitated and then decided Ruth was safe to tell. "We are trying to figure out who killed Jerianne."

Ruth replied, "And why? I'm wondering if she found some clues as to who killed my sister and that got her killed."

CHAPTER 19

Early morning mountain shadows lay heavy across Cooke City's downtown district. Lynn and Winnie had driven down to Sweet Stuff in Jake's jeep with several boxes of freshly crafted candles to restock shelves. Lynn was lucky enough to find a parking space almost in front of the shop, and Ruth was holding the door open while she and Winnie carried the boxes. They had barely gotten them inside when Detective Palmer entered the shop and stood just inside the door.

"Good morning," Lynn called out, then saw the grim expression on Palmer's face and froze.

Ruth and Winnie looked over and stared at the detective, who was the picture of exhaustion and something more, something that looked a lot like bad news.

"Mrs. Cranston, would it be possible for me to use your office for a few minutes?" Palmer asked without explanation.

"Of course," Lynn responded.

Palmer crossed the shop to the open glass doors and went into the Sugar Shack, not saying another word. The three women exchanged perplexed looks and turned to watch his progress through the crowded dining area. Palmer approached Jeremy Walsh and bent down, murmuring in his ear. When he pulled back, Jeremy rose from his chair at the table where several regulars were gathered. Together, they left the diner, and Jeremy followed Palmer into the back area of Sweet Stuff. Palmer closed the door behind them.

They heard the men's lowered voices but were not close enough to catch their words. Ruth made it as if to inch closer to the door, but Lynn shook her head, and Ruth stopped. All three jumped as a loud crash reverberated through the walls.

"What the …?" Winnie started to say.

Jeremy slammed the door open and burst out of the office area, his face ashen. Without pausing, he rushed across the shop and left, not quite closing the door behind him. Palmer came out and gazed in the direction Jeremy had gone.

Turning to face the three women, his face lost all expression. "At about 3:30 a.m. this morning, the body of Chad Chandler was found on Soda Butte Creek by a couple of tourists. He had been stabbed to death. At this point, I cannot say more."

Palmer walked slowly across the floor and exited without another word, leaving Lynn, Ruth, and Winnie equally speechless.

"Dear God," Lynn finally muttered.

"I don't think He had anything to do with this," Winnie replied drolly.

Ruth blinked. "Wait. Tourists found Chad at 3:30 this morning. Really? What were they doing down on Soda Butte Creek at that ungodly hour?"

Winnie snorted. "They're tourists. Who knows."

Lynn turned to gaze into the Sugar Shack, where the morning batch of tourists and regulars were blissfully unaware of the drama.

"So, who wants to be the bearer of bad news today?" she intoned.

Ruth and Winnie looked at each other.

"Flip you for it," Ruth quipped.

"Nah, let's both go," Winnie responded. "Coming, Lynn?"

Lynn shook her head. "You guys go do the honors while I call Jake."

Shaking her head, she watched as they marched in lockstep through the wide opening to the Sugar Shack before turning to use the phone behind the checkout counter.

Jake was shocked into silence by Lynn's news. Then he exclaimed, "What the hell is going on? First, Jerianne, now Chad. I don't know what to think."

Lynn agreed. "Me, either. It could be the same killer, or maybe Chad killed Jerianne, and Jeremy killed Chad? Or something entirely different. Palmer was not forthcoming. He asked to use the office and brought Jeremy in from the Sugar Shack. They had some sort of altercation, after which Jeremy rushed out of there. Palmer shared the bare minimum information and also left. And he looked awful. I'm betting he was called in right away and has been up for hours."

Jake hesitated, then declared, "I'm coming down there. You are going to need help. When I get there, take Winnie to her home for a few hours. It's not good for her to be agitated after the head injuries she suffered."

Lynn chuckled grimly. "I don't know about that. She seems to be holding up well."

Jake grunted. "Anyway, I'm on my way. There is no way I'll be able to concentrate on projects after this news. See you in a few minutes."

Lynn busied herself to set up the free coffee service, then started unpacking the new candles and finding space for them on the shelves. It helped me have something positive to do. She was about halfway done when Jake came in. Right behind him were a family and several other customers, followed by Old Lucy.

"Where's Ruth?"

Lynn glanced up. "She and Winnie are in the Sugar Shack sharing the news. It's been really quiet since they went over there."

Jake nodded. "Well, I'm going to bring her back. I suspect we will have a lot of business in a very short time."

Lynn left the unpacking and went to help customers. Ruth and Winnie returned and promptly got to work as well. When Lynn asked Winnie if she wanted to go home, Winnie was adamant that she preferred to stay.

"Okay, if you think it's not going to be too hard on you," Lynn reluctantly agreed. "Let's call Julie and let her know to feed Miss Elsie and bring in the mail. You and I can drop by over there this afternoon, okay?"

Winnie lost no time dialing her neighbor and regaling her with the news. Lynn sighed. Poor Chad, she thought. And poor Jeremy lost both his love and his friend in less than three weeks. What was this town coming to?

Later, when they had eaten a light supper and were relaxing by the fire, Jake leaned close to Lynn and asked, "Did you notice who was in the Sugar Shack this morning?"

Lynn thought about it. "Well, Jeremy, for sure. But I don't recall seeing Kevin Montgomery or Paul Davidson. Or Lucinda Russell, for that matter. A few of the regulars and a lot of tourists. You know, now that I think about it, I didn't even notice that Chad wasn't there."

Jake frowned. "And Palmer said tourists found Chad at 3:30 this morning on the creek? What were they doing out there?"

Lynn smiled weakly. "As Winnie said, they're tourists. Go figure."

Jake was silent for a while. Then he said, "You know, I think we need to know more about Chad. We barely glanced at his social media. I believe it might help to get a clearer image of him. And yes," he added as Lynn sighed, "I hate digging into other people's business, but under the circumstances, it might help us understand a little more about Chad and possibly his relationship with Jeremy."

"Do we really want to do this?"

Jake nodded. "It's not a matter of 'want.' It may be a matter of self-preservation. There's a murderer in Cooke City, and we're right in the middle of this mess."

Lynn and Jake waited until Winnie wished them a good night and then went off to bed before starting their research. With the laptop balanced on her lap, Lynn began keying in questions and was rewarded with more information than she expected.

"Well, first on Tik Tok, Chad has a podcast focused on the gay community, which isn't a surprise," Lynn commented. "He had thousands of followers, and I suspect he was earning some income from his popularity. He was outspoken about gay rights."

Jake grunted.

A few more sessions with the keyboard and Lynn added, "Okay, at home in Chicago, Chad performed regularly at several of the trans clubs. He seems to have been quite popular for his outrageous comedy and also for promoting other performers. "

Jake said, "That must be how he supported himself unless he had a day job. But I'm inclined to doubt that because he wouldn't have been able to just leave for the entire summer as he did last year and now half of this summer."

Lynn continued to search. "I'm not finding a family. Perhaps Chandler isn't his real name? Chad Chandler sounds like a stage name. Should I be checking for arrest records?"

Jake pondered, then agreed. "To the extent that you can, probably a good idea."

Lynn speed-typed more into her laptop, "Huh. I just found a solid connection. Chad was arrested three years ago for leud behavior and alleged extortion. Guess who his attorney was."

Jake stared at her. "Jeremy Walsh?"

"Good guess. You are correct."

Lynn scanned the monitor, reading down through a short newspaper article that appeared in the Chicago newspaper's police blotter.

"Kind of run-of-the-mill but Jeremy got him off on a technicality. They didn't even make it to court," Lynn murmured. "Chad must have been grateful. It says he was drunk, got into an altercation with a club show customer after hours and then allegedly attempted to blackmail him."

Jake started. "Okay, suppose… just suppose… Chad tried to blackmail someone here? I mean, how can he afford to rent a place for the entire summer on what he probably makes?"

Lynn added, "And he picked the wrong person."

Jake finished, "Jerianne's killer."

CHAPTER 20

Once again, Sweet Stuff was barely opened when Detective Palmer pushed through the front door. Lynn looked up from the checkout counter and smiled at him.

"You look a little more rested this morning," she greeted him.

Palmer snorted. "Very little. Now, here's the thing: I am asking for some assistance from you."

"Okay," Lynn replied tentatively.

"We found Chad Chandler's sister, living in Schaumberg, which is a suburb of Chicago," he continued. "Chandler's real name is Wilbur Larson. She has asked that we have Chandler cremated and the ashes sent to her. I'm assuming there are no plans for a funeral here as of yet."

Lynn understood immediately. Chad hadn't been all that popular. The brash, outspoken attitude he had adopted, possibly as a defensive mechanism, held most people at bay.

"I haven't heard it mentioned," Lynn confirmed. "That takes the pressure off. But am I guessing Jeremy Walsh might want a memorial service?"

Palmer shook his head. "I haven't spoken to Mr. Walsh since yesterday morning. He glanced into the Sugar Shack. "And I see he's not here this morning. Have you or your colleagues seen him since then?"

Lynn looked across the store to Ruth, who was working with a couple of customers. Ruth shook her head. Winnie had wandered across to the Sugar Shack and was seated at the counter. She seemed to be in a deep conversation with Connie Russell.

"I don't think so. Do you think he left town?" Lynn asked.

"I know he hasn't," Palmer stated firmly.

Lynn shrugged. Of course, they were watching for him in the pass and the park gateway. "Okay, I'll spread the word that there probably won't be a funeral, but I think it might be helpful to give Jeremy a chance to decide," she said. "After all, Chad was his friend."

Palmer grimaced. "And that's another avenue I haven't had time to explore. Any insight on what that relationship was?"

Lynn thought about it for a moment. "Jeremy is heterosexual, and Chad obviously is not. Jeremy told Jake and me he had asked Jerianne Baker to marry him. There's just too many possibilities."

Palmer nodded. "Exactly the same conclusion I've reached.

Lynn added, "I guess Chad and Jeremy met a couple of years ago when Jeremy represented him after he had been arrested for attempted extortion."

Lynn stopped short, suddenly aware she had given away more than she intended.

"I see you've been doing a bit of investigating on your own," he commented. "Need I remind you to be careful? We are dealing with either one or two killers here. And it might be that the two murders aren't related."

Lynn started. "I didn't think of that possibility. But you are right; we can't afford to assume anything. Trouble is, with a population of just 77 people, excluding tourists, that makes for a troubling situation."

Palmer agreed wholeheartedly, accepting the fact that he might be looking for two murderers in the tiny town.

"Well, duty presses. Just please, watch yourself, your husband, and your friends," he warned. "I've got my plate too full now to take on another case."

With that, he mock-saluted her and strode out of the shop.

Lynn looked at the closed door for a long moment, then called out to Ruth, "I'm going next door for a few minutes."

She crossed the shop and walked through the sliding door opening. The Sugar Shack was bustling this morning, every table filled. Lynn worked her way to where the regulars were sitting at their usual table.

"Good morning," she greeted them in a low voice so as not to be overheard by the tourists. "The police have just informed me that Chad Chandler will be cremated, and his ashes released to his sister in Illinois. This seems to eliminate a funeral. Has anyone here heard from Jeremy about what he would like to do?"

The group, which included Lucinda McDonald, Kevin Montgomery, and Paul Davidson, among a couple of other residents, was silent.

"I, for one, wouldn't have gone to his funeral anyway," Lucinda said with a grim expression. "I'm not going to miss that snarky little SOB, and I'm fairly sure a lot of others won't either."

Lynn was quite taken aback. Lucinda saw her expression and continued, "Chad habitually attacked us all verbally. His jabs were cruel and, sadly, painfully on point most of the time."

Kevin nodded. "Yeah, the only one he was easy on was Jeremy. I got tired of fending off his vicious little remarks. I finally just ignored him."

Paul added, "Me, too. Chad was obnoxious. I never figured out whether he was jealous about Jeremy or being defensive, or that was just how he communicated."

Lucinda snorted inelegantly. "Chad was a weasel. Somehow, he seemed to know exactly what buttons to push to make a person feel crappy about themselves. At times, I was ready to backhand him a good one.”

Lynn shook her head slowly. “I had no idea. But what about Jeremy? Has any of you seen or heard from him since yesterday?”

They all shook their heads.

“I suppose at least one of us should check with him. He’s renting a small cabin between here and Silver Gate,” Paul said.

Kevin stood up. “I’m headed that way now; got a job to estimate in Gardiner. I’ll stop by and get in touch with you later.”

“Thanks, Kevin,” Lucinda replied. I hope he’s okay. Jeremy is a good guy. I hate what’s happening to him. I don’t pretend to understand how he tolerated Chad, but he didn’t deserve to lose Jerianne and Chad like this.”

Lynn went back to Sweet Stuff, wondering about the reactions of Jeremy’s friends. They were totally supportive. Not a hint that they thought he was involved in any way.

When Winnie followed her back to Sweet Stuff, they decided to leave Ruth in charge and take Winnie home. That way, she could visit with her cat, Miss Elsie, and her neighbor Julie for a few hours, giving her a break from the need to stay at the shop. They had no more gone into Winnie’s home when Palmer pulled up in his squad car.

“Just the person I wanted to see,” Palmer called out as he climbed out of the car.

He waited until he was inside Winnie’s home and seated with the three women in the kitchen to break the news.

“I got the toxology report on the medicine we removed from your bathroom,” Palmer began. “The lab found a lethal level of rat poison mixed into a bottle of cough medicine that had already been opened and partly used.”

"Oh, my God," Julie breathed. "Winnie! That's awful!"

Lynn and Winnie were stunned and silent.

"Mrs. Fredricks, have you remembered anything from the night you were attacked?

Winnie shook her head. "No, I keep trying to remember. The last thing I can recall is leaving the Timberline Inn and walking toward my car. It's all blank until I came to alone at the lookout."

Julie said, "Winnie, you can stay with me if you like."

Winnie started to decline but Palmer held up a hand. "It might be a good idea to not stay in the same place all the time," he explained. "I don't like endangering you, Mrs. Harper, not at all. But at this point, I don't want things to be too predictable."

Lynn suddenly realized another danger. "Winnie, the murderer still has your keys. Have you or Julie eaten or used any of the food here?"

Winnie and Julie both stared at her. "Oh, my… we had coffee the other day with creamer from the refrigerator," Julie whispered.

Palmer said, "I advise you to dispose of all the food in the fridge and anything that can be adulterated in the cupboards. We won't test it all that way, and it will ensure you are safe."

Julie exclaimed, "Let's do that right away, Winnie. It won't take long to clear out the fridge. I suppose anything canned or sealed will be okay, right?"

Palmer nodded. "Just don't eat anything with the seal broken."

Palmer left, and Lynn walked back to Sweet Stuff. There was a lull in the shop, so Lynn caught Ruth up on all that was happening.

"I'm wondering if you can help Jerianne's sister and me pack up her personal things from the cabin so they can be shipped to Belinda's home."

Ruth didn't hesitate. "No problem. What if we do that when Jake comes in this afternoon? It's been relatively quiet this afternoon. We can call Belinda and set up a time."

Lynn agreed and made the call. They arranged to meet Belinda at the cabin with an assortment of empty boxes at 3:45. Then Lynn called Jake not just to catch him up on all the happenings of the morning but also to let him know he would be alone at the shop for a few hours.

"Is Palmer any closer to solving this?" Jake asked.

Lynn sighed. "No, he's just as puzzled as we are. I think the idea of moving Winnie around is a sound one. I hate to think of someone sneaking into the house and poisoning all of us."

Jake snorted. "Fat chance with Mickey here," he chuckled. "The whole town would know."

Lynn laughed. "Yup, they would. Anyway, see you around 5:30 or so at Sweet Stuff."

Lynn and Ruth arrived at Jerianne's cabin just moments before Belinda. Jerianne's sister pulled a ring of keys from her purse and unlocked the cabin's front door. Stepping inside, all three stopped in shock. The cabin looked as if a tornado had ripped through it.

CHAPTER 21

After a shocked and silent moment, the three women carefully stepped back through the door and onto the porch.

"I'll call Detective Palmer," Lynn said, pulling her cell phone from her purse.

Upon hearing that Palmer was already on his way to Cooke City for another matter, the dispatcher told Lynn she would contact him about the break-in. They stood on the porch for another minute or two before Lynn suggested they wait for Palmer on her porch. Once there and seated where they could see him coming, Lynn called Jake and filled him in on what they had found. Jake offered to close up and join them, but Lynn demurred.

"It's okay. We don't know when this happened, but I'm fairly sure it was more than a few hours ago, possibly last night," she pointed out. We'll be okay. We called it in and are waiting for Palmer to arrive."

Jake reluctantly agreed. "Just be careful, okay?"

Nearly an hour passed before Palmer drove up. Lynn, Ruth, and Belinda walked across the yards to meet him on the cabin's porch. Before Lynn could say anything, Old Lucy slunk out from behind the cabin and crowded close to Lynn's legs. When Palmer took the keys from Belinda and opened the cabin's front door, the fur rose on her back, and the low rumble of a growl emanated from her. Palmer's eyebrows rose. When she opened the door, Old Lucy's growl turned into a nasty snarl, and she stalked inside.

"Hmmmm, I believe she recognizes the scent," he commented. "Too bad she can't tell us who it belongs to."

Palmer stood just inside the door and looked around. Then he reached for his radio and messaged the dispatcher to send the crime lab team. Without touching anything, he carefully skirted the immediate area by the door and slowly walked through the cabin. Coming back outside, he shook his head.

"Someone was looking for something," he stated.

Belinda said, "You mentioned that Jerianne's laptop and cell phone are missing. Did you find any written notes?"

Palmer turned to study her. "No, we didn't."

Belinda nodded. "Okay, because Jerianne always made written notes as backup when she was interviewing by telephone or researching. Rather than take a chance on missing or forgetting anything, she wrote it down and then transcribed it to files on her laptop. Jerianne got that idea from a friend who worked as a newspaper reporter. The friend called them her alibi files."

Palmer thought for a moment. "Any idea where she might have kept those notes?"

Belinda shook her head. "No, but I do recall that she mostly worked in the kitchen area and on the back porch. Knowing Jerianne, they were probably close to those areas."

While they were talking, Old Lucy slipped out of the door and sat down beside Lynn, who absently mindedly rubbed her head, and scratched her ears. Calm now, the shaggy dog sighed and leaned into her legs.

Belinda sighed deeply as well. "I was hoping to get things packed up and shipped, but I believe it's going to be a while. Do you mind if I go back to the hotel and we try again tomorrow … if that's okay with you, detective?"

And Ruth also was ready to leave. "I think I'll go home now, Lynn. By the time they get here and go through all this mess, it's going to be too late to accomplish anything. Do you mind? I'll help out tomorrow for sure."

Lynn and Palmer shook their heads. The two women walked off together toward Cooke City's main street.

"Do you need me here," Lynn asked.

"Not really," Palmer replied. "You are going back to Sweet Stuff?"

Lynn said, "Yes, Jake is holding down the fort alone, and it's still early."

Palmer added, "And where is Mrs. Fredricks?"

"She's staying at her neighbor's house… Julie Parker's… for the night."

"Okay, I'll catch up with you later, after the team is finished. Either here at your house or at Sweet Stuff."

The business was surprisingly brisk at Sweet Stuff when Lynn and Old Lucy arrived. Jake looked a bit frazzled and relieved to see them. Old Lucy left Lynn's side and walked slowly across to the checkout counter, where she had begun to curl up on an old rug when she was in the shop. She liked sleeping under the counter and out from under the feet of the tourists.

"How bad was it?" Jake asked.

"Pretty messy," Lynn replied. "I didn't get a chance to look in the other rooms, but the living room and dining area were totally trashed. Worse, it looked like someone didn't just search the cabin. It looked as if whoever did this deliberately destroyed a lot of Jerianne's possessions. A lot of her beautiful pottery was broken, books ripped up, that sort of thing."

Jake whistled softly. "That sounds like a lot of anger."

"Poor Belinda. We were going to pack up what she wanted to keep," Lynn murmured as two customers approached the checkout. "Now she won't have much to remember her sister by."

Just before closing, Palmer came into Sweet Stuff and headed straight in their direction. The store had quieted for the evening, and the final customer was on her way out.

"Well, whoever did this went out of their way to damage as much as they could," Palmer confirmed.

"Were you able to find Jerianne's notes?"

Palmer shook his head. "No sign of them. That doesn't mean they aren't still there somewhere. Just that we didn't find them in all the obvious places."

Jake said, "You checked under the bed and behind the toilet?" with a deadpan expression.

Palmer smirked. "Yup. And I would really have liked to find them. We are frankly working on next to no clues right now. We need a break."

And that gave Lynn an idea.

The next afternoon, Lynn and Ruth met Belinda at the cabin. This time, there were no rude surprises, but the cabin still looked like a disaster area. Painstakingly, they sifted through the rubble, finding items Belinda wanted and wrapping them in towels before packing them into two medium-sized boxes. They also filled several large garbage bags with items Belinda didn't want to take, as well as all the broken things. When they had done all they could, Belinda signaled she was satisfied.

"I'll have time to ship these tomorrow morning before I start for home," she said. "I can't thank you two enough."

Lynn gave her a hug. "I know how difficult this must be for you. I just wish we have some resolution to all this. But we can keep in touch if you like."

Belinda smiled. "I would like that very much."

Ruth added, "Me, too…"

"Absolutely," Belinda said.

Lynn took a deep breath. "And if you agree, would you be willing to leave the cabin keys with me? I know the landlord will want them back, but I can hold them for him."

Belinda gave her a curious look.

"I just want a chance to look for those notes," Lynn confessed. "If there is any chance at all they are still here, it would be wonderful to find them."

Belinda frowned. "You're playing detective? Oh, Lynn, please be careful. This person is dangerous. You have two murders in less than three weeks, probably committed by the same person."

Ruth added, "Not to mention that awful attack on Winnie."

Belinda nodded. "That's right. Promise me you will be careful. Bring Ruth with you, or Winnie so you aren't here alone. Please?"

Ruth agreed. "That's a good idea, Lynn. I'll help any time you need me."

Belinda handed over the cabin keys, front door and back, before leaving with Ruth to walk back to the town center.

Lynn gazed down at the keys and sighed.

"Let's hope you are the keys to some answers," she whispered to herself.

CHAPTER 22

Jake and Lynn opened Sweet Stuff early the next morning. It was an August Sunday, deep into summer tourism season, and they anticipated steady business. Ruth had asked for the day off to attend a family reunion in Gardiner, an annual event, so they were on their own. Lynn prepped the checkout counter while Jake set up the complimentary coffee table.

Joining Lynn at the checkout, Jake murmured, "Did you notice? It looks like things are back to normal with the Sugar Shack breakfast crowd."

Lynn looked across the store and into the busy diner where its owner, Connie, was holding court from behind the counter. "Yup, they're all there."

Jake grinned. "The usual suspects."

Lynn groaned. "At least it's good to see Jeremy getting back into society. He hasn't been around for days."

As the number of customers increased, Lynn and Jake kept busy answering questions, finding products, and checking out. Winnie came in with her neighbor, Julie, and stayed to help until mid-afternoon. The day passed swiftly. Shortly before their 8 p.m. closing time, Jeremy Walsh sauntered into the nearly empty shop. He glanced across at the sliding glass doors that separated the shop from the Sugar Shack.

"Good, it's closed. I wanted to talk to the two of you," he stated.

Jeremy turned to gaze at the piece of art still hanging in its prominent place. "I need to measure that artwork. Kevin and I were going over plans for the remodel of that old log house on the land I bought. I want the perfect place to hand this."

Jake dug around in a drawer behind the checkout counter and found a tape measure. Going into the storage area, he returned with the ladder and set it up close to the art. Jeremy pulled a small notepad and pencil from a pocket in his jacket.

"Let's see," Jake said. "Top to bottom, it's 36 inches."

Jeremy made note of that while Jake climbed down to measure the width.

"Here, let me hold one end of the tape," Jeremy offered.

"Okay, its 52 inches wide," Jake announced. "And its depth is 3 inches, not counting the elkhorn."

"Got it," Jeremy replied. He looked wistful. "God, I wish Jerianne had seen this. She would have loved it as much as I do. The old house has a magnificent fieldstone fireplace, but I don't plan to hang this on it. I'm afraid of smoke or heat damage. I have a safer spot picked out in the area that will be for dining."

Lynn said softly, "I'm sorry about Chad."

Jeremy turned to her with a rueful smile. "Thank you. I miss him. I grew up an only child. Chad was like a kid brother. We became friends when I represented him in court a few years back."

Lynn commented, "I cannot imagine anyone wanting to hurt him."

Jeremy grunted. "I can," he responded. "Chad didn't have filters. And he was viciously observant. He noticed everything. And he didn't cut anyone any slack. He could be downright obnoxious."

Jake added, "Still... "

Jeremy nodded. "I defended Chad in a case of assault and attempted extortion. I got him off, but I'm more than certain he was guilty. It wouldn't surprise me to discover he had tried to blackmail the wrong person... again." Jeremy was thoughtful for a moment.

"It's funny, I lost both Jerianne and Chad within three weeks. And that's the only thing they had in common."

Jake said, "And what was that?"

Jeremy gave a half laugh. "They were both acutely observant. You know, Jerianne was working on a writing project. She wouldn't tell me anything about it, said it would 'jinx' it."

Lynn studies him. "But you have an idea."

Jeremy nodded. "Yes, I do. Several months ago, your employee came into the Sugar Shack to get a sandwich for lunch. I guess she forgot hers at home, and Connie gave her a hard time. Well, anyway, when Ruth left, I think it was Lucinda who said something about Ruth's sister being a cold case."

Lynn and Jake exchanged looks. "Go on," Lynn encouraged him.

"Paul was at the table, and Lucinda asked him if his son had gone to school with Ruth's sister… what was her name? Oh, Anne Marie. Anyway, Paul and his family live in Gardiner, as did Ruth's family."

Jake asked, "And what did Paul say?"

Jeremy replied, "Only that his son, Brian, was older than Anne Marie and was out of school when her murder occurred. I noticed how intent Jerianne was. I mean, she didn't say a word or ask a question, but I could tell she was intrigued."

Jeremy wished them a good night and left. Jake and Lynn waited until he was out of earshot before Lynn said, "Well, that confirms what we were speculating about."

Jake nodded. "It sure does."

Lynn added, "And that makes me even more convinced that we need to search Jerianne's cabin and see if we can find those notes

Belinda told me about. I'm betting someone else was looking for them as well."

Jake answered with, "I hope whoever it was didn't find them."

After a quick supper, Jake and Lynn along with a leashed Mickey, walked across the twilight lit lawn and unlocked the front door to Jerianne's cabin. Almost before they could step inside, Old Lucy glided up the porch steps and slipped in before them, her growl a low hum.

"Goodness!" Lynn exclaimed. "That dog seems more wolflike every day!"

Jake paused in the middle of the living room area and said, "So, what are you thinking? I mean, where do you want to look?"

Lynn replied, "Belinda, Ruth, and I went through every room thoroughly. I think maybe the kitchen. That's where Belinda said Jerianne liked to work… as well as on the back porch."

The two made their way into the small kitchen with its tiny two-person dining table. Lynn stood in the middle and turned full circle, a thoughtful look on her face.

"We went through the cupboards and drawers," she mused. "The refrigerator and freezer are empty."

Jake asked, "Did you look on top of the cupboards?"

Lynn brightened. "No, we didn't. Good idea!"

Jake pulled one of the kitchen chairs close to the bank of cupboards and carefully climbed on top. From his raised vantage point and with his height, he could see the tops of all the cupboards as well as the top of the refrigerator.

"See anything?"

"Nope," Jake said, stepping down and replacing the chair. "What are you doing?"

Lynn was bent over, peering under the table. "Just wondering if there's a handy hiding place here," she muttered. "How about under the drawers?"

Old Lucy scratched at the back door.

Jake frowned. "What, you can't go out the front? The door is open."

Then, it was Lynn's turn to frown. "Hmmm, Belinda did say Jerianne liked to work on the back porch when the weather was nice. Let's take a look."

She flicked on the back porch light and unlocked the door. Outside in the darkening night, the porch was shrouded in shadows. A beat-up old kitchen chair and a small footstool stood off to one side. A ratty, faded pillow was propped in the chair's seat. On the other side was a rough wooden bin stacked with firewood. Old Lucy wandered over to it and began sniffing at it. She looked at Lynn and whined.

"Hmmm, that's odd," Lynn murmured.

She stood in front of the bin, her hand rubbing Old Lucy's back. Tentatively, she reached out and pulled a log from the top, then another. She gasped, then pulled two more and dropped them on the porch floor. Reaching in, she pulled up a plastic garbage bag. She opened the top and peered inside.

"Bingo!"

She handed the bag off to Jake and carefully replaced the logs. Jake started to pull his cell phone from his pocket.

"What are you doing?" Lynn demanded.

"Calling Palmer," Jake replied. "We need to notify him right away that we found Jerianne's notes."

Lynn shook her head. "No, we don't. It's late. We can call him in the morning."

Jake glared at her. "You just want to read this before we hand it over."

"Damn right I do," Lynn argued. "We can call Palmer in the morning. Ruth is opening up, so we will both be home until I go in at 11 a.m. That way, no one hanging around the Sugar Shack will know what we found."

Jake sighed. "Lynn…" he began.

"Awww, come on, Jake, I know you want to know as much about what's in here as I do. And if we hand it over right away, we won't get it back or even know what Jerianne found out," Lynn wheedled. "

Jake reluctantly agreed. They locked up the cabin and went home. But it was a long time before either one slept.

CHAPTER 23

"Do we or don't we?"

Jake put the garbage bag-wrapped packet in the middle of the kitchen table and placed his cell phone beside it.

"I believe we must," Lynn responded. "The police will use this for their investigation, but they don't know these people as well as we do."

Jake nodded. "True, possibly, but how well do we actually know them?"

Lynn grimaced. "Apparently not as well as we should and need to. How can we protect ourselves as well as our friends if we just give this unseen to Palmer?"

"So we are in agreement," Jake answered.

Gingerly, he opened the plastic using only two finger tips, and pulled out a stenographer's notebook. While he did that, Lynn got up from the table and found a ruled notepad and pencils in one of the kitchen drawers.

"Ready?"

"Whenever you are," Lynn replied.

Lynn removed a large rubber band that was marking the page where Jerianne had left off, lifted the cover of the notebook, and scanned the hand-written notes.

"I'm assuming this is in chronological order," Lynn commented. "She starts with what looks like a synopsis of the police report on Anne Marie's murder investigation, along with notes from old newspaper articles. She found a whole lot more than we did online."

Jake said, "Sounds as if she drove over to Gardiner and went through the newspaper's archives, plus visited the police department personally."

Lynn started at the top left. "Okay, Jerianne starts by noting that the murder of Anne Marie had to have something to do with a resident of Gardiner and not a tourist, which makes sense. Oh, interesting. We know Paul Davidson's son Brian was a little older than Anne Marie and had evidently already graduated. But this says Paul was also the Greggory family's insurance agent."

Jake said, "That's a double connection right off the top. It's reasonable to think Brian would at least have known who Anne Marie was, but now we know it's likely Paul knew as well."

Lynn nodded. "Right. Oh, and remember Ruth telling us her sister told her she was gay? Jerianne found out about that somehow."

Jake frowned. "But how?

Lynn thought about it for a moment. "We need to keep in mind that Jerianne worked as a waitress, not just at Sugar Shack but also at the Timberline Inn. Think about all the inadvertent comments she might have overheard."

Lynn scanned the pages further and then started. "She notes that Chad was making crude remarks about Kevin Montgomery, something about his business ethics."

Jake's eyebrows rose. "Wouldn't Jeremy be aware of anything like that? He hired Kevin to rebuild the property he purchased. And what would that have to do with Anne Marie's murder?"

"Nothing, probably, but possibly a sideline theme. Or perhaps… we could ask Ruth if Kevin did any work for her family. I believe Kevin lives in Red Lodge now, but his business has to cover a vast area."

"Good idea," Jake said. "At least we can ask her. It's not like we can interrogate the others. They don't know us that well."

"True," Lynn replied. "Jerianne has a list of potential suspects down the left side and across from it, a synopsis of the pertinent evidence taken from all the reports. Interesting."

Jake grinned, "You mean all the usual suspects?"

Lynn laughed outright, "Yes, and a few more we don't even know." Lynn flipped another page and gasped. "You have to see this."

She held the notebook where Jake could see the "Connie + Paul?" notation that filled more than half a page inside a heart. They both stared at the paper.

"Whoa, didn't see that coming?" Jake murmured.

Lynn sighed. "Me, either. And I find it hard to believe. I mean, we see them almost every day in the Sugar Shack, and I've never noticed any kind of relationship other than a very casual one. Not that we've ever paid close attention, that is."

"It's either very hush-hush because Paul is married, or possibly it's one-sided," Jake finally stated. "But you know, if there were anything remotely overt, Chad might have noticed it as well."

Lynn grunted. "Do you think it's serious enough that it got both Jerianne and Chad killed? I mean, Chad has a history of blackmail. And when I was in the Sugar Shack right after Chad was murdered, Lucinda McDonald referred to Chad as a 'snarky SOB.' It sounded as if she had a run-in with Chad as well."

Jake shook his head. "We have more than enough suspects for both murders. Jerianne because she might have decided Paul was responsible for what happened to Anne Marie, and Chad because he possibly tried to blackmail the wrong person. But which person?"

Lynn added, "Or persons. Palmer said he might be looking for two murderers. Oh, bother. This stuff," she exclaimed, indicating the pile of Jerianne's notebooks, "is making it worse instead of better."

Jake further complicated the issue. "Don't forget about Winnie," he reminded her. "She must have figured out or overhead something that nearly got her killed. So, was it about Connie and Paul? Winnie is fairly chummy with Connie. Or was it about the old murder case?"

Lynn groaned. "I'm going to cheat and skip to the last page. And darn… Jerianne doesn't draw any conclusions at all here. It's like a television program that ends with 'to be continued.' This whole thing is giving me a massive headache. I vote we quit."

Jake agreed but added, "Still, we need to be observant as well, and perhaps someone will give his or herself away. Meanwhile, we stay close and try to keep Ruth and Winnie safe."

"Ruth?" Lynn asked.

"Yes, remember she was hanging out in the bar at the Timberline, watching Jeremy's drinking party, which included all of the suspects," Jake replied.

"Ouch."

Jake rewrapped the notebook in the garbage bag and carried it over to the sink, where he placed it in an adjacent drawer and covered it with dish towels. Both looked up as there was a scratching noise at the door. Jake crossed the floor and opened it. Old Lucy squeezed inside and slunk over to the table, where she plopped down next to Lynn. Mickey raised her head, her stumpy tail knocking on the floor.

Lynn reached down and scratched Old Lucy's ears and was rewarded with a sigh of contentment.

"Thanks, old girl," Lynn whispered. "We might not have found Jerianne's notes without you."

Jake commented, "And I'm not certain whether or not it was a good or bad thing."

"That's okay,' Lynn said. "At least we have a clue what to watch for now."

Early the next morning, Jake phoned Palmer and informed him that they had found Jerianne's notebook. They ate breakfast and then sat at the table drinking coffee, the notebook placed uncomfortably between them. When Palmer pulled up and knocked, Lynn let him in.

"Here you go," Jake said as he handed Palmer the wrapped book. Palmer looked at it and then at the two of them.

"I don't suppose the two of you could resist peeking inside," he asked.

Lynn replied, "You would be right. But it didn't clear up much of anything."

Palmer sighed. "I knew it was too much to ask that you not touch it. But I also know you are concerned for your safety, and I won't mention this to anyone. Please also do not tell anyone you found it. Your lives may depend on that."

Palmer left. Lynn checked the time and rose from the table to get ready for work. She needed to be at Sweet Stuff at 11 a.m. Jake followed her upstairs and also started getting ready to go out.

"You're not staying to work on that new project?"

Jake sighed. "Nope. We stick together until this is resolved. The artwork can wait. It's not a commissioned piece, so there's no deadline. And I can put together some frames at the store to supplement what we have in stock."

Lynn added, "Okay. And Winnie's coming back here for a few days as well, to give Julie a break. Hopefully, Palmer will get enough from the notebook to solve the case, but I doubt it."

Jake nodded. "Somehow, I doubt it as well."

CHAPTER 24

Jake and Lynn arrived at Sweet Stuff with Mickey to find Ruth and Winnie in total control and enjoying it. At 11 a.m., the shop almost always had customers browsing. They were either the after-breakfast bunch or the pre-lunch bunch. Lynn took a few minutes when no one was paying attention to study the diners in the Sugar Shack. The usuals… Jeremy, Lucinda, and Kevin… apparently had left for the day. However, Paul Davidson was seated at the counter, watching Connie work and occasionally exchanging comments.

"Hmmmm," Lynn murmured to herself. "It looks purely innocent."

But half an hour later, Palmer and two uniformed deputies entered the diner. Lynn called Jake out of the back, where he had been cutting wood for picture frames. Together, they watched as the officers approached Paul.

"That was fast," Jake whispered.

Lynn shivered. "He must have wasted no time working on Jerianne's notebook."

It was so quiet in both stores that they could easily hear what was being said in the Sugar Shack.

"Paul Davidson? I'm Detective Palmer of the Park County sheriff's department. Would you please come with us?"

Paul rose and faced them. "Am I under arrest?"

"No, Mr. Davidson, we would like to question you about the deaths of Anne Marie Greggory, Jerianne Baker, and Chad Chandler."

Paul slumped on his stool. "I had nothing to do with any of those deaths," he stated. "Where are you taking me?"

Palmer replied, "Sir, we will be going to the sheriff's office in Livingston."

Paul stood up, pulled a cell phone out of his suit coat pocket, and asked, "Can I call my family? What about my car?"

Lynn and Jake didn't hear their answers as the officers and Paul moved away from the open doorway and toward the front of the diner.

"Hmmmph," Ruth muttered from behind them.

"Well, that certainly is going to stir things up," Winnie commented. "I wonder what set that off?" When no one said anything, she continued, "Connie is really going to be upset."

Lynn turned to look at her friend. "What do you mean?" she asked with what she hoped was an innocent expression.

"Connie is obsessed with Paul," Winnie answered. "Has been for years."

Lynn murmured, "I thought he was married."

"Oh, he is and has no intention of changing that," Winnie smirked. "The worst case of unrequited love I've ever seen. Oh, he knows she's sweet on him. How could he not? But to give the man credit, he has never once taken advantage of it."

Across the store, Connie stood behind the counter with a dumbfounded expression. When the door had closed behind Paul and his escort, the tourists all began talking at once. The two waitresses who had been standing stock still when they came in began working again.

"I wonder what put them onto Paul Davidson," Ruth said from behind Lynn.

"Do you think he had anything to do with your sister's murder?" Lynn dared to ask.

"He was one of a few I suspected," Ruth replied with a sigh. "But to tell the truth, he was down a ways on the list of suspects.'

Lynn prompted, "Who are the others?"

Ruth touched Lynn on the arm and signaled with her head that she wanted to talk privately in the stock room. Lynn followed her into the room and shut the door.

"Okay, one of the reasons I moved to Cooke City was to try and figure out who killed my sister," Ruth confessed. "I love my job here, but I'm mainly here to find that person and see that justice is being done. But I haven't been able to find enough evidence that clearly points to any one person."

Lynn waited patiently while Ruth decided what she wanted to share.

"Paul is one. Kevin Montgomery is another. He was around that spring. My parents hired him to rebuild an outbuilding damaged by a falling tree that April. I didn't see anything obvious, but Anne Marie was a beautiful young woman."

More moments went by.

"And Lucinda Russell is another."

Lynn was startled. "Lucinda?"

Ruth nodded. "I believe I told you Anne Marie had come out to me as being gay. Lucinda is, as well. I distinctly recall running into her several times in Gardiner when Anne Marie and I were shopping for groceries around the same time. In fact, it got a little weird how often we did run into her. We also seemed to run into Paul's son, Brian, more often than not."

Ruth continued, "All that was before Jerianne and Jeremy met. And, of course, Chad wasn't a suspect, except I did wonder if he might have killed Jerianne out of jealousy. Anyway, please don't say anything to anyone about this. I am afraid of being a target like Winnie."

Both of them jumped at the soft knock on the stock room door. Jake opened it wide enough to stick his head in and ask, "Can I come in now?"

Ruth and Lynn nodded. "We were just coming back out," Lynn said.

Back in Sweet Stuff's shopping area, they went back to work helping customers. Lynn glanced into the Sugar Shack and saw Winnie seated at the counter, consoling Connie. "This is why Jake and I dare not say anything about finding Jerianne's notes," Lynn thought, and sadly added Connie to her list of the usual suspects.

Jake, Lynn, and Winnie locked Sweet Stuff up at 8 p.m. and, with Mickey, walked the few blocks to their home. Along the way, Old Lucy drifted out of the gathering darkness and joined them, drawing curious looks from the tourists still on the streets. After a light supper, they took mugs of fresh coffee out onto the porch. The three mostly sat silent, lost in their thoughts and speculations.

"Blue car."

Lynn jumped. "What?"

Winnie repeated, "Blue car. For some reason, I keep seeing a blue car."

Jake murmured, "In connection with what?"

Winnie sighed. "I'm not certain, but I believe I'm starting to remember … at least little flashes."

Lynn asked, "What do you remember about it?

Winnie replied, "It's driving away in the dark, but I can see the color, light blue and the taillights."

"So, who owns a light blue car?"

Jake grunted. "Too many people."

Winnie actually laughed out loud. "You got that right."

Lynn added, "Like suspects. We seem to have too many of them."

Jake said, "We can eliminate a few."

Winnie agreed. "Like Jeremy Walsh. He was in love with Jerianne, and Chad was his friend. I'm not sure why."

Lynn nodded. "True. So, not Jeremy Walsh. What about Lucinda Russell?"

Winnie started. "Lucinda? Really? I didn't know she was a suspect. Besides, she lives too far away to be coming here in the middle of the night, which is when both Jerianne and Chad were murdered."

"Point taken," Lynn murmured. "Let's take Lucinda off the list."

Jake said, "Okay, how about Kevin Montgomery? Doesn't he live in Red Lodge? That's a four-hour drive unless you cut over Beartooth Pass. Same issue as Lucinda. He lives too far away."

They sat silent for a few minutes.

"What about Paul? Do you really think he killed all three of them?" Winnie asked.

"No, I don't," Lynn averred. "I can't see Paul hauling Anne Marie's body two miles from a trailhead and hiding it in a coulee, do you? And both Jerianne and Chad were killed by someone who was extremely angry. I don't believe Paul has it in him."

Jake stared at her. "So, do you know who the killer is?"

Lynn nodded. "I'm not sure who killed Anne Marie, but I am very much afraid I do know who killed Jerianne and Chad and assaulted Winnie."

Winnie gasped. "Well, don't keep us in suspense, Lynn."

Lynn stood up and said, "Let's go inside. A pot of fresh coffee, and I'll explain why I think I know."

Jake called Mickey in from the sideyard. The little Corgi was reluctant to obey, and Jake grew impatient. "Come on, Mickey. It's too dark to see anything lurking out there. Let's get inside."

Mickey finally trotted up on the porch, and they all trooped through the front door together. Mickey immediately burst into a loud series of sharp barks that stopped them in their tracks.

Standing in the middle of the living room was Connie Russell, and she had a gun pointed directly at them.

"Some watchdog you are, Mickey," Jake muttered.

CHAPTER 25

"Connie," Lynn murmured. "How did you get in?"

Connie smirked. "The back door was unlocked. Very careless of you."

"And to what do we owe the honor of this visit?" Jake said.

Connie waved the gun in the direction of the dining room table. "All in due time," she stated. "For now, please sit at the dining table and put your hands on the table."

Jake nudged Lynn and glanced down at his shirt pocket where his cell phone was tucked.

"Hey, Connie, how about we make a pot of coffee and sit down like civilized folks to talk," she suggested, turning away from Jake to head toward the kitchen area quickly. She took several steps with Connie staring at her, startled, before Connie reacted.

"Stop right there," Connie demanded. Turning along with Lynn, she again indicated the dining table.

Meanwhile with Connie's attention focused on Lynn, Jake was able to pull the cell from his pocket and key something into it. He dropped it back just as Connie looked back to see if he and Winnie were following. They sat at the dining table, the three on one side with Connie standing, facing them from across it.

"Okay, so what is this all about?" Lynn asked softly.

Connie snorted. "As if you didn't know," she accused Lynn. "I know you got Paul arrested, and he's innocent! Paul is a saint! He would never hurt a single soul."

Jake cleared his throat. "Connie, Paul was just taken in for questioning. He hasn't been arrested or accused of anything yet."

And Winnie added, "What do you think he was arrested for, anyway?"

Connie almost screamed, "The murder of Anne Marie Greggory, Ruth's sister, of course."

Lynn frowned. "Why would you think he had anything to do with that?"

"Because he lived there. He knew Anne Marie," Connie replied. "And whenever her name comes up, he turns white and looks frightened."

Lynn sighed. "That doesn't really mean he was involved. Maybe the police think he might have some information because of his proximity and the fact that he knew the family."

Connie glared at Lynn. "And how did you know that?"

Lynn shook her head. "You might as well know this now. Jake and I found Jerianne's written notes. We turned them over to Detective Palmer this morning. Did you know she was looking into Anne Marie's murder with the idea of writing a novel?"

Connie grunted. "I suspected it when she took an early afternoon to drive over to Gardiner. And it's all your fault, Winnie."

Winnie started as Connie's gun was suddenly pointed at her. "What do you mean, me?"

Connie answered, "You remember sitting at the counter, talking to me about doing some personal investigation after Jerianne's murder? You said there were rumors that Jerianne was researching an old murder case someone had mentioned. Paul was sitting right behind you, and he overheard. He got up and left right away."

Winnie glared back at Connie. "And is that why you attacked me?"

Connie had the grace to wince. "I didn't want to, Winnie. And I just couldn't kill you, either. We've been friends for so many years… but I didn't want Paul implicated in any way."

Winnie was growing increasingly agitated. "Oh, but it was okay to bash my head in and leave me up in the mountains to die of exposure?"

Jake intervened. "Ladies, let's calm down here. There's no need for this. Connie, why don't you tell us why you are here and what you hope to achieve with this confrontation."

Connie's face became exasperated. "It should be obvious. I want Lynn to drive me to Livingston as my hostage."

All three of Connie's hostages looked dumbfounded.

"I don't understand," Lynn finally stammered.

Connie snorted. "It's simple. We go to Livingston, where I exchange you for Paul."

Winnie started to say something, but Jake elbowed her.

"And do you really think that will work?"

Connie lost what little patience she had left. "Yes, of course, it will work. They won't want anything nasty to happen to Lynn. Nor do you, Jake."

Jake responded, "I see. And what will you do after Paul is released?"

Connie said, "We'll take the car and go somewhere where they can't find us."

Under the table, Jake tightly gripped Winnie's arm, hoping this would keep her from saying anything to provoke Connie further. It was clear to him and to Lynn as well that seeing Paul taken into custody, even for just questioning, had sent her over the edge.

Lynn took a deep breath and asked, "Connie, did you kill Jerianne?"

Connie replied, "You know I did. I suspect you've known for a while now. You're not stupid. And how could I let her ruin Paul with her infernal digging into his past?"

Jake and Winnie were stunned by Connie's frank admission of the murder. Lynn steadied herself and continued with her efforts to keep Connie talking.

"Would you tell us what happened the night Jerianne died?" she asked.

Connie took a deep breath. "I went to Jerianne's cabin to just talk to her and try to convince her to drop the hunt for Anne Marie's killer. But she wouldn't listen. She said it was important for Anne Marie's family to finally know what happened, even if it were in a fiction novel. She planned to turn everything she found over to the police when she was finished with it."

Lynn ventured, "What happened?"

Connie muttered, "She just wouldn't listen. We were in the kitchen area. I saw a knife laying on the table and grabbed it. Jerianne tried to run away. She got almost to the front door and staggered out onto the porch. I stood over her and made sure she was dead."

Lynn asked, "And did you take her laptop and cell phone?"

"Of course," Connie said. "I knew anyone could find all that information off her laptop and trace her calling records. But I didn't know about the written notes until I overheard Jerianne's sister mention her habit of keeping both computer and written information."

Lynn nodded. "And that's when you went back to the cabin and searched it again."

Connie sighed. "So, where were they?"

"In the wood box on the back porch," Lynn said.

Connie shrugged. "Jerianne was smart. I would have never thought of that."

Lynn took another deep breath. "And what about Chad?"

Connie actually burst out laughing. "That asshole? He thought he could blackmail me."

Jake asked, "What for? Did he know that you killed Jerianne?"

Connie grimaced. "No, it was actually worse. So observant, that conniving little jerk. He threatened to tell everyone that Paul and I were having an affair, that we were lovers. It's totally false. Paul loves his wife. He cares deeply about his entire family. And he respects the fact that I am in love with him without taking advantage of it. I told you, he's a saint. But Chad didn't care about that."

Lynn prodded a bit more. "So what happened then?"

Connie explained, "I agreed to meet him at 2:30 that morning. No one would think twice about me being out because I start baking at 3 a.m. We were to meet by the creek, where it was unlikely any tourists would be wandering around. I took a knife from the Sugar Shack's kitchen with me. I just walked up behind him in the dark and stabbed him."

Lynn was nearly in tears. "Oh, Connie, I'm so sorry."

"Don't be. I'd do anything for Paul," Connie replied. "He would have been the love of my life if he hadn't already been married when we met. He's too honorable to do anything that would compromise his marriage. And I can do no less than honor his commitment."

At that moment, there was a sharp knock on the front door.

"What the…!" Connie exclaimed.

Jake, Lynn, and Winnie sat frozen at the table. The knock came again. Connie waved the gun at Jake and said, "Answer the door, but don't try anything stupid. Do you understand?"

Jake nodded and rose carefully. He walked across to the door and opened it a crack. With his back to the room, no one else saw his look of amazement and relief. Slowly, he opened the door, and Detective Palmer stepped into the room, closing the door behind him.

CHAPTER 26

"Well, what do we have here," Palmer commented, taking in the scene fully with a glance."

Connie immediately aimed her gun at Palmer. "Detective, remove your weapon and drop it on the floor."

Instead, Palmer raised both hands and said calmly, "How about you drop your gun, Ms. Russell?"

Connie snorted and aimed the gun directly at Jake's cheset.. "Now. Drop your gun, or I will shoot Jake."

Lynn gasped. Winnie started to speak, but Jake laid a hand on her arm.

"Okay, I'll drop my gun," Palmer said quietly.

No one moved as Palmer unsnapped his gun and lifted it with two fingers.

When he let go, it clattered on the hardwood floor. Then he once again held up his hands.

"Please put down the gun. There is nothing you can do to change what is going to happen," Palmer said in a reasonable tone.

"I want Paul Davidson released immediately," Connie demanded.

Palmer shook his head. "Sorry, that won't be possible."

Clearly becoming more agitated, Connie replied, "Why not? Paul is innocent. He didn't kill Anne Marie."

Palmer nodded. "True, Paul Davidson did not kill Anne Marie."

"Then why are you still holding him?" Connie growled.

Palmer sighed. "He may not have been directly involved in her death, but he knew from the beginning who was responsible."

While he was speaking, Palmer had inched slowly closer to the table.

"Stop right there, no closer," Connie ordered. "So what? He didn't do anything wrong."

"Actually, he did break several laws," Palmer contradicted. "Paul admitted that his son, Brian, killed Anne Marie."

Connie argued, "So Paul was protecting his son, so what?"

Palmer remained calm. "Paul will be charged for failure to report a death, desecration of a dead body, obstruction because he lied or failed to inform the police of a felony or who committed it, among several other charges."

"Nonsense!" Connie yelled, waving the gun wildly.

"Careful, Ms. Russell, we don't want any more people injured or killed, now, do we?" Palmer stated as he took another step closer.

Connie glared at him. "Lynn, come here. Now."

Jake started to rise, but Connie pointed the gun directly at him and shouted, "Sit down! Lynn, I said, come here."

Reluctantly, Lynn stood up and moved slowly to stand next to Connie, who immediately moved behind her and shoved the gun against the small of Lynn's back.

"Now, Detective Palmer, contact the sheriff's office or whoever and tell them to release Paul, or Lynn will suffer the consequences," Connie said.

"You're not going to hurt Lynn," Winnie stated. "Lynn hasn't done anything to deserve this. She has always been your friend, not like Jerianne and Chad."

Jake added, "And I suspect you didn't want to hurt them, either."

Connie responded, "Well, maybe not Jerianne, but the late and unlamented Chad got exactly what he deserved." She thought for a moment. "How did you know I was here, detective?"

Jake answered for Palmer. "Easy. Let me show you," he said, carefully pulling his cell phone from his shirt pocket. "You see when you weren't looking, I hit the emergency 911 app… the police have been listening to this entire conversation."

Connie was incensed. "How clever of you, Jake."

"Not really," Jake replied modestly.

Holding out his cell phone as if to show her the screen, Jake started to get up. At the same time, Palmer took two fast steps forward. Without thinking, Connie swung the gun to cover Palmer. Instantly, Lynn turned and grabbed Connie's arm, jerking it upward and away from the two men.

"No!" Connie screamed.

Jake and Palmer started running around the table's ends to where the two women were struggling. But before they could reach them, a gray blur launched itself out of the kitchen and smashed into Connie's back. She went down on the floor, pulling Lynn down with her. The gun came loose and skidded across the floor. Lynn rolled away from Connie, staring at a viciously snarling Old Lucy, whose huge canine teeth were around Connie's neck.

Behind the women, a sheriff's deputy with pistol drawn inched into the dining room, looking totally bewildered. Palmer picked up Connie's gun and set it on the table.

"Easy, Lucy," Lynn crooned to the still-growling dog. "It's okay, girl. You can let her go now. Easy now."

Slowly, the big dog pulled her teeth back from Connie's neck, but she remained straddling the terrified woman. Palmer reached down and cautiously snapped handcuffs on one of Connie's wrists while Lynn continued to coax Old Lucy off to one side.

Not to be left out, Mickey casually strolled up to the prone Connie and licked her face. Lynn couldn't help it. She burst out laughing, as did Jake, Winnie, and Palmer.

When Jake could finally stop, he muttered once again, "Some watchdog you are."

Palmer and Jake helped Connie to her feet, and the deputy joined Palmer to escort her out of the front door. Lynn followed behind and was aghast at the sight outside the house. At least six squads and a SWAT wagon were spread across the driveway and lawn. Other squads had the road blocked on both accessways. And, of course, beyond them, dozens of residents and tourists were crowded in groups.

"Jake wasn't kidding," she murmured. "Everyone in town must have heard his cell phone."

CHAPTER 27

"Oh, my God, I'm so glad it's finally over," Ruth gushed as Lynn unlocked Sweet Stuff's door the next morning. "I always suspected it was Brian Davidson but never had enough proof. Besides, he and his father lied to the police."

As Lynn motioned Ruth and Winnie to go ahead, and stepped inside the shop herself, Old Lucy slipped in and trotted to her place under the counter.

"Why did you know it was Brian?" Lynn asked, but without any real desire to know.

"First, Brian was fixated on Anne Marie. Second, he talked about wanting to be a park ranger in Yellowstone and was planning to go to school. Plus, Brian hiked a lot in the park. He likely would have known about the area where Annie Marie's body was found."

Lynn responded with, "Hmmmm."

She was saved from talking about the past night when several tourists came into the store and began browsing. With a lightness and friendliness Lynn had not seen before in her employees, Ruth cheerfully greeted them and asked how she could help.

Sighing deeply, Lynn opened the sliding doors between Sweet Stuff and the Sugar Shack, then wandered across the shop and perched on a stool behind the checkout counter. There, her gaze gradually shifted to the Sugar Shack, which was open and doing gangbuster business. She really hadn't wanted to come in this morning, but Jake had convinced her that it wouldn't be as bad as she believed.

"The quicker we get back to our routine, the better we will feel," Jake had insisted.

Easy for him, Lynn thought grumpily. He stayed home to work on the project that had been side-tracked by the murders and the need to protect Winnie. Staring abstractedly into the Sugar Shack, she abruptly realized that Jeremy Walsh was looking directly back at her, a sympathetic expression on his handsome face.

Much to her surprise, Jeremy left his table of friends and strolled nonchalantly into Sweet Stuff, where he helped himself to the courtesy coffee Ruth had brewed.

"Good morning," Jeremy said, approaching the counter and saluting her with his coffee cup.

"Is it?" Lynn felt churlish saying it but somehow believed Jeremy would understand. Suddenly, she couldn't hold back the resentment she was feeling about what the past weeks' events had done to strip away her sense of security and happiness. "Nothing will ever be the same."

Jeremy smiled, but sadness lingered around his eyes. "Oh, I agree wholeheartedly. Things will be different. But it doesn't necessarily mean it will be a bad different."

Lynn sighed, "I shouldn't complain. You lost far more than I. We survived, the situation was resolved, and no one else was hurt. I don't know why I feel so out of sorts."

Jeremy nodded. "Understood. I'm guessing you and Jake came here after years of hard work and stress, built up the kind of business you have always dreamed of in a place where it felt like nothing could ever go wrong. Sadly, no such place exists."

Ruth slid behind the counter to ring up customers' purchases. Lynn moved out of her way, walking around the counter to join Jeremy. They walked to a quiet corner of the shop.

"Well, one good bit of news: Sam has announced he is making an offer to buy out Connie in the Sugar Shack," Jeremy said. "He's been working for Connie for 12 years and feels confident he can run the business. I've offered to help him financially by buying a half-interest in the diner as a silent partner."

Lynn managed a wan smile. "That is good news. I was concerned that the diner would close, and I wasn't sure how it would impact our business. It's a huge draw."

Jeremy chuckled. "You can stop worrying about that. Sam has promised that he knows how to make Connie's famous huckleberry bear claws. The aroma should be filling up the shop any time now."

Lynn found herself actually laughing.

"That's what I like to hear," said a familiar voice behind them.

Turning, Lynn and Jeremy found Detective Palmer standing nearby. "After last night, I was worried about you, but there wasn't any time to talk to you," Palmer added.

Lynn replied, "It's okay. It was hectic."

Stepping closer, Palmer studied her closely. "I hope you are going to be okay. Jake and Mrs. Fredricks as well. I'm mainly here to let you and Jake know that Connie Russell will be assessed to see if she is fit to stand trial. There is a strong case for an insanity plea. Either way, she will not be released on bond, not with two counts of murder and one of aggravated assault and unlawful restraint."

Jeremy responded, "That's a relief."

"Also, we have arrested Paul and Brian Davidson. They are being processed as we speak," Palmer added. "I don't have any more to share about them at this time."

Palmer held out his hand. Lynn shook it, grateful that he had taken the time to let her know she and Jake were safe.

"You probably won't have to witness, just a deposition," Palmer continued. "I'll let you know when."

Jeremy and Lynn watched him leave Sweet Stuff.

"Feeling a little better?" Jeremy asked.

"Yes, as a matter of fact, I do," Lynn confessed. "Palmer answered a lot of the questions that have been nagging me. The knots seem to be slowly coming untied."

Jeremy nodded. "Good. Remember, you have a lot of good friends here, and you are surrounded by a lot of decent people., Don't let this destroy all you've worked so hard for."

Winnie wandered in from the Sugar Shack and gazed after Jeremy as he left. Then she turned to Lynn and said, "He's right, you know. You and Jake have a lot of friends here in Cooke City. It's not good to let one person spoil everything you've worked so hard for. You still have all of us."

By late afternoon, when Winnie and Ruth had left for the day, the Sugar Shack was closed, and Jake had joined her; Lynn was feeling more like herself. Jake noticed, of course.

"It's going to take time, but I know we're going to be okay," Jake affirmed. "We didn't make a mistake in choosing Cooke City. Things like this happen every day and everywhere. But I believe it's extremely unlikely anything like this will ever happen again here."

Jake wrapped his arms around Lynn and hugged her tight. At that moment, Lynn chose to believe he was right.

THE END

---

www.ingramcontent.com/pod-product-compliance
Lightning Source LLC
Chambersburg PA
CBHW050525160726
48003CB00001B/459